"You have to get up, Zach," Ava whispered urgently. "I'll help you."

He nodded painfully and pushed himself to his hands—no, just one hand; she saw his left arm was broken—and knees. He was broad and several inches over six feet tall. All of which meant he'd outweigh Ava by a sizable amount. Nonetheless, she tucked herself under the crook of Zach's uninjured arm and said, "Okay, let's do it."

They fought their way upright. His weight had her wanting to crumple, but she kept lifting. "That's it," she encouraged.

Zach lurched to his feet and his eyes met hers. He bit out, "Now...what?" before clamping his jaws together again. Shudders rattled his entire body.

"Down toward those trees. I have a tent we can set up."

As they staggered through the snow, Zach's shaking came in waves, receding, then gripping his body again. Ava tried to time it so they could pause. If he went down, she wasn't sure she'd be able to get him up again.

HIGH MOUNTAIN TERROR

USA TODAY Bestselling Author

JANICE KAY JOHNSON

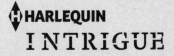

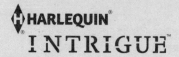

Recycling programs
for this product may
not exist in your area.

ISBN-13: 978-1-335-59041-1

High Mountain Terror

Copyright © 2023 by Janice Kay Johnson

Harlequin Enterprises ULC
22 Adelaide St. West, 41st Floor
Toronto, Ontario M5H 4E3, Canada
www.Harlequin.com

Printed in U.S.A.

An author of more than ninety books for children and adults with more than seventy-five for Harlequin, **Janice Kay Johnson** writes about love and family and pens books of gripping romantic suspense. A *USA TODAY* bestselling author and an eight-time finalist for the Romance Writers of America RITA® Award, she won a RITA® Award in 2008. A former librarian, Janice raised two daughters in a small town north of Seattle, Washington.

Books by Janice Kay Johnson

Harlequin Intrigue

Hide the Child
Trusting the Sheriff
Within Range
Brace for Impact
The Hunting Season
The Last Resort
Cold Case Flashbacks
Dead in the Water
Mustang Creek Manhunt
Crime Scene Connection
High Mountain Terror

CAST OF CHARACTERS

Ava Brevick—A nature photographer, she's dismayed to find she's not alone in the snowy mountain landscape. Another snowshoer seems to be pursuing her and armed men on a ridge above her must have crossed the Canadian border illegally. Operating on instinct, she photographs them...only minutes before a monstrous avalanche breaks free to roar right down the mountain at her *and* her pursuer.

Zach Reeves—A cop intent on finding solitude snowshoeing in the backcountry, he too is stunned to find he's far from alone. Is it possible the internationally sought terrorist Zach's border patrol friend warned him to watch for is among the heavily armed crowd on the ridge? Time for spec op soldier Zach to reemerge. The gutsy woman who saves his life needs him, given the pack of Russian terrorists intent on hunting them down.

Grigor Borisyuk—Proud of his reputation, a ruthless assassin and a fanatic for his causes, Borisyuk doesn't tolerate mistakes—and being seen and photographed by a woman who could give away his presence in the US means going to any length to eliminate her before she can share that picture.

Chapter One

In her rare glimpses of the sky, Ava Brevick marveled at the stunning blue, made richer by the contrast with snow, ramparts of rock and the deep green of the forest cloaking the North Cascades Mountains.

Picking her way among the infuriating tangle of willow and alder near the river and having to watch for the fallen trees and rocks hidden beneath the snow, Ava hadn't been able to maintain anything close to the pace that was possible on a stretch where snow lay smoothly on top of a trail maintained during the summer. Her snowshoes felt clumsy right now, almost more trouble than they were worth. This was nothing unexpected; even during the kinder time of year, most of the Cascade Mountain wilderness didn't welcome two-legged intruders.

After unsnagging her snowshoe from a whip thin stem that was part of a thicket she thought was alder, she paused for the second time in the past ten minutes to look cautiously behind her.

She'd been alone out here in this snowy expanse for two days now. Trails in the park were closed during winter—and May was still very much winter high in the mountains. A respected wildlife and wilderness photographer, Ava had been dropped by helicopter to work her magic, seeking the extraordinary moment when sun slid through a snow-laden branch or glanced off water dancing between the ice and rocks. She hoped to capture some good photos of the animals that weren't hibernating—or would be emerging from hibernation anytime. Not given to feeling lonely, she loved what most people would say was profound silence, but which to her ears was filled with the crack of a far-off branch, the whisper of wind, the occasionally ominous settling of ice and snow on steep slopes, the high cry of a bird or the scream of a small creature that had just become prey.

She'd already captured enough images she thought would delight the organization that had funded this expedition, but planned to set up another blind this evening in hope more nocturnal animals would wander her way. There were plenty of those deep in the Cascade Mountains, from mountain beavers and porcupines to the red fox, as well as the northern saw-whet owl she had yet to glimpse.

For herself, the only predators to fear in these mountains up by the Canadian border were grizzlies, reintroduced into the Cascades some years back, or an unusually aggressive black bear. She felt pretty confident neither would be emerging from hibernation just yet. Mountain lions could be a threat on rare occasions; she kept a sharp eye above when she passed below a tall rock upon which one might crouch. But a world without other humans was one where she relaxed her usual wariness.

What unnerved her now was the suspicion she *wasn't* alone out here anymore. It was like walking through a dark alley, certain you heard footsteps behind, except they stopped when you did…only, a fraction of a second too late. Someone was behind her, and fleeing would do no good. She couldn't exactly hide, given the conspicuous track she left in the snow, and if she parted from the almost-path following the bank, she wouldn't be able to bull her way through the rampant growth. Unfortunately, the dense vegetation kept her from seeing who might be back there.

She had heard a helicopter yesterday, although she didn't see it and had no reason to think it had landed. When the sound of the rotors had faded until silence reclaimed the wilderness, she'd dismissed any worry. Park rangers might keep an eye on the land they guarded with an occasional flyover.

But if it *had* dropped someone off, it had been a distance away, and how had he—or *they*—gotten close enough behind her that she heard the swish-swish of snowshoes and thought she'd gotten a glimpse of movement? And no, there weren't a lot of alternate choices of paths around here, not with the steep flank leading up to a sharp peak on her one side and the rock-and ice-strewn river to her other.

If she stopped, would he? If she decided to turn around to go back, would he nod and politely let her pass?

She was being ridiculous; why would anyone want to sneak up on her?

She didn't know whether to be glad or sorry that the trail was parting away from the river now and climbing above a jumble of huge boulders deposited by long-ago slides or avalanches, now surrounded by a clump of evergreens she identified as western red cedar, Sitka spruce and hemlock. Sunlight ahead dazzled her eyes as she emerged into the open.

The way was easier here, and she achieved a smooth stride in her snowshoes even as she continued to gain elevation and evaluated this open bowl of land. Now she had another cause for nerves: avalanche danger was high in this country, and it looked as if the trail led her across a curved, open slope she'd guess slanted at a forty-or forty-five-degree angle. She didn't have an awful lot of experience with winter dangers, but anyone with common sense could see that the long-broken tree trunks poking jaggedly out of the heavy snow weren't a good sign. An avalanche had plunged down this chute in the not so distant past. And yes, the warming conditions—although the day felt damn cold to her—contributed to the danger.

Still, she could see a clear line with the snow lying differently where the summer trail stretched across the way ahead. A single person stepping lightly wouldn't put any significant stress on the weight of snow, ice and rocks higher up.

Except now she felt exposed because of that uneasy feeling that she was being pursued.

A couple of minutes later, Ava couldn't resist stopping and turning. She'd been right. There he was, just emerging from the trees near the frozen river bank, moving fast and with surprising grace, climbing effortlessly to close the distance between them. She saw it was a big man wearing a dark green parka and carrying a huge pack. Only three or four hundred yards separated them.

Foolish instinct said to run, but her attention was abruptly jerked away from him when, out of the corner of her eye, she spotted movement high on the forested ridge across the river from her. To her shock, in an open stretch that had to be the result of a wildfire, a group of men were silhouetted against the blue sky. To her naked eye, they were nothing but small figures that didn't belong there, at least this far north. There was no trail heading down that ridge, summer or winter, Ava was quite sure of that. What's more, they were moving southbound, strung out, picking their way slowly. On snow-shoes? She couldn't tell.

Habit had her lifting her camera with the enormous lens that she always had ready hanging around her neck. She snapped off the cap and zeroed in on them, until she saw them as if they were startlingly near, if still very small. They all wore white, including their packs. Or something like white capes draped over the packs? Most had carriers of some kind slung over their shoulders, too, although those were black. Could the group be skiers dropped off by helicopter? She couldn't imagine that kind of commercial venture was permitted within the national park. Besides, they were nowhere near an elevation high enough to be above the tree line. No slope *could* be skied in this vicinity, and she was pretty sure there wasn't one on the other side of the ridge, either.

Suddenly apprehensive, she stared at the sharp image of the man in the lead. Distant as he was, even through her lens, she was shocked to see that he held a rifle, one with a shape that had become all too familiar from constant news reports about mass shootings and war. That had to be something like an AK-47, not a typical hunting rifle—and, anyway, hunting was banned in the national park.

Not even sure why she was doing it, she took photos, moving from one man to the next. A couple of them wore what were probably fleece balaclavas. Several didn't, or had pulled them down. Maybe the sun felt warmer up there, she thought in some distant part of her mind. Those faces she saw clearly, and she photographed them without conscious thought.

Several of them had come to a stop while she studied them. At the same instant, she saw the glint of sun off glass and knew someone up there was looking back at her.

Men carrying automatic weapons, men who shouldn't be where they were, were looking at her.

She hastily let the camera drop and snatched

up her poles. Apprehension made her want to turn around and race back toward the trees, nearer if she went back instead of forward, except the stranger was closing in fast on her now.

Go, she thought.

She broke into a near run, wishing futilely that she was on cross country skis instead of the far clumsier and slower snowshoes, but that had never been possible in this difficult terrain.

Go, go, go!

ZACH REEVES HAD spent the past couple of hours speculating on who could be out here in the remote wilderness he'd expected to have to himself. He'd looked forward to cutting his own tracks in the snow.

Call him selfish—he'd *wanted* to be alone. The whole point of this expedition had been to escape the pressures he felt from coworkers, neighbors and crowds at the mall or competing with him for a corner table at the café. After ten years as a spec ops warrior, he wasn't adjusting well to normal life.

Life on the military base between operations had been fine, if not his favorite. He'd always managed during his rare visits home to Minnesota where his sister and brother lived. Now, he almost wished he'd gone to work as a Washington state patrolman or sheriff's deputy who patrolled miles of roads instead of the job he'd taken as a detective for the Whatcom County Sheriff's Department. The work was more interesting, but on patrol he'd have been covering a lot of empty country in the rural county, likely going hours at a time without having to interact with anyone.

This was Zach's vacation, damn it. He'd sought solitude and found a way to achieve it. It was bad enough that he had company, but what in *hell* was a woman doing out here alone?

Given the hefty pack she carried, it had taken him a while to realize the snowshoer ahead of him was female, but he no longer had any doubt. How had she gotten into this remote area, unreachable by road at any season or by trail in what was still winter in the North Cascades? Who did she think would bail her out if she got into trouble? He sure didn't have cell phone service in this deep vee between a high ridge and a higher mountain. He supposed she might carry a satellite radio, as he did.

He evaluated the white slope above before breaking from the trees to climb after her into a bowl carved in the ridge. He knew an avalanche path when he saw one; in July or August, wildflowers and shrubs would dominate in the sunlight, free of the tree cover he'd been traveling through. He'd have avoided this stretch if he could, but a couple of snowshoers were unlikely to tip the balance to bring the icy monster down on them.

Zach raised his head to see that the damn woman had stopped dead, lifted an enormous camera and was staring up at the ridge above the river. Now what? Zach flicked his gaze the way she was looking, and his muscles locked. His radar jumped into the red.

He hadn't heard a helicopter in the past day since his drop-off. Those men almost had to have crossed the Canadian border to get here, and this route wasn't ever an approved border crossing. Right now, with the border patrol stretched thin and on high alert to watch for a known terrorist sneaking into the country, that group had to have slipped in, taking advantage of the remote countryside that couldn't be adequately monitored. They must have expected to stay cloaked in dense, northwest forest, except that a wildfire had burned that cover in the past year or two.

He had razor-sharp vision. Even without lifting his binoculars, he recognized the weapon the guy at the front carried. A flash of light up there had him blinking; the sun must have reflected off the lenses of binoculars. Had they noticed him yet, or were they watching her?

Either way—

A very faint crack that might have been a gunshot came to him. From this distance, that wouldn't have been a concern, but a flash of fire arced across the sky.

A rocket-propelled grenade. He was racing toward the fool woman in front of him even as he evaluated what he'd seen and knew they hadn't fired directly at her.

No, they had a better way to kill a lone traveler who'd seen them.

An explosive burst came from the slope above the two of them on this side of the river. For one instant, nothing changed but for the white puff where the shell had landed. The sound of a second shot came to him. Before he had a chance to react, an enormous crack began to split open in the surface of a thick layer of snow and ice at the top of the slope, at first moving in slow motion in each direction.

Even before Zach saw the increasing speed the crack spread across the slab, he shouted, "Avalanche! Get out of the way!"

She gave a startled look at him, then up.

A loud *whuump* came from the sliding slope.

He wouldn't get to her, he realized in the compartment of his brain that kept him making logical decisions under fire. Couldn't help her, anyway. None of the old-growth trees with their massive boles had survived in this gully to provide shelter. He wouldn't make it out of the path, either. Farther ahead of him, she might reach the edge of the avalanche zone if she put on the burners.

A boulder ahead provided the only hope. It wasn't large enough to protect him, he knew, but he saw no other possibilities and raced to throw himself behind it.

Then he curled low, braced his pack against the cold rock and waited for one of the most brutal forces of nature to smash into him.

SHE RAN, cursing the need to lift each foot high to clear the snowshoe from the snow. It was as if she were moving in slo-mo even while the monstrous white slab fractured at what seemed a leisurely pace. She knew, *knew*, that appearances were deceptive. Snatching a quick look, she saw in horror that a mass almost as wide as this open bowl of land was gathering speed as it first slid, then thundered into motion down the slope. One last look at the guy behind her. There he was one instant, the next he vanished behind a boulder. Lucky guy. Her thighs burned, her breath whistled. A roar drowned out everything else.

It hit her like a semitruck on the freeway, slamming into her even as it tossed her, flipped her. A last instinct had her wrenching at the handle on the chest strap of her pack. Then her thoughts became nothing coherent. She had the terrifying sense she was upside down as she saw her snowshoes snatched from her feet to disappear in the white tsunami. Her poles were long gone. Winded, Ava flailed for a grip on anything at all, her hands finding nothing. She had to be screaming, but the sound was too puny to be heard even by her own ears. It was like leaping off an Olympic ski jump and not coming down. Weightless, she was flying, but also being buffeted from every side. It hurt, it hurt, it hurt.

THE NEXT THING she knew, she lay still. Astonishingly, when she shook her head, she saw a sliver of light. Had she lost consciousness? She had no idea. Something was choking her, and she gagged. Her legs felt as if they were encased in concrete that she prayed hadn't quite hardened yet, but her arms—yes, she could move them, although it was a struggle. Her groping hand found a flap of nylon, blue rather than the green of her pack. Avalanche airbag. *Oh, thank God, thank God.* She'd remembered to pull the rip cord. It must have inflated immediately, creating a brightly colored pillow that acted to make her more buoyant, lifting her toward the surface.

She broke through the snow and saw sky. The airbag had worked. Fumbling, she discovered her camera had been whipped around her head, and it was the strap throttling her. Awkwardly, she untwisted the camera strap from around her neck. It was a miracle she hadn't lost it. How damaged it was… Not important.

Now she just had to find a way to crawl free from the hardening snow.

She kicked and flung handfuls of snow away, widening the hole around her shoulders and head. One glove was gone, she saw, but she didn't even feel the cold. That wasn't a good sign, but if she couldn't dig herself out, what was a little frostbite?

It couldn't have taken more than a couple of minutes. It felt like forever before she found herself on her hands and knees, facing downhill. Her pack weighed her down, but the fact that it hadn't been torn from her body had saved her life. Would save her life again. She couldn't whip out a phone and call for help. She hadn't even brought an avalanche beacon, because she'd known that, isolated as she'd be in the back country, no one would come in response. With a sleeping bag, tent, food and more clothes, though, she could survive. She could.

She let out a cry. She was alive, but what about *him*? Ava had quit caring why he was following her; he was a fellow human being. He'd yelled a warning to her, hadn't he?

She staggered to her feet and looked at the devastation around her, frantically trying to orient herself. She'd ridden the avalanche almost to the end, but what about him? He'd started slightly lower than her, but right in the center of the chute. The boulder. Where was the boulder?

It took her a minute, and that was a minute he couldn't afford. In preparing for a trip in Alaska a couple of years ago, she'd read the horrifying statistics: someone who was really buried would start to lose consciousness in only four minutes from breathing their own carbon dioxide. The odds of surviving even after being dug out decreased dramatically as the minutes ticked by.

There! she thought. All she could see was a faint curve of rock surrounded by the tumble of snow and ice, but that had to be it. She didn't remember seeing any other boulders so high above the river.

She scrambled the distance to it on her hands and feet and even knees.

"Can you hear me?" she yelled.

Nothing. No, something stuck out of the snow. Ava tugged it out. A snowshoe. *Oh, my God.* He had to be near, didn't he?

She called out again, waited for an answer, tried over and over as she dropped her pack and unzipped it with fingers too numb to want to cooperate. She'd bought the airbag at the urging of mountain-climbing friends, but otherwise hadn't planned much for an avalanche.

"I'll be careful," she'd told everyone.

Famous last words.

For whatever reason, she'd added a folding probe to her gear. At last she pounced on it. By accident, she spotted her other gloves and hastily, gratefully changed. Then she unfolded the long probe, stood and began stabbing it into the snow. The chances of her finding him weren't good. If he'd been swept too far to the left or right of the boulder, she could poke the probe into the snow for days and not find him. If he was buried too deep…

Ava didn't even want to think about that.

She prayed as she'd never prayed before, and stabbed the probe repeatedly into the avalanche debris.

Chapter Two

Hell of a thing, to die here and now, on vacation, after surviving countless firefights and bombs, silent raids and HALO jumps from aircraft in every war-torn part of the globe.

Zach's struggles slowed. He might as well be in a casket six feet under for all the good kicking and battering with his shoulders and fists had done. It wouldn't take long to burn up all available oxygen.

His mind drifted. He tried to slow his breaths but knew how useless that was. The woman. Was there any chance at all she'd survived? He hoped so. For all his irritation that she was out in this wilderness where he'd wanted to be alone, she'd moved well, as if she knew what she was doing.

Damn, he was cold. He struggled a little more to prevent himself from freezing solid, even if keeping himself from stiffening up wouldn't do a thing to change his fate.

Something poked him. Had to be his imagination, unless…? It poked again. And then he'd swear he heard a voice calling to him, even if he couldn't make out words.

"I'm here!" he bellowed, the effort causing darkness to swim in front of his eyes.

Then all he could do was lie there and wait: for rescue, or for death.

AVA SCRAMBLED BACK to her pack and pulled out the folding shovel. Back at the probe she'd left standing in the snow, she started to dig. The probe might have struck a rock or a solid chunk of ice. It could have been anything. But she gambled. If this was him, she might get to him in time. Otherwise—

No, she had to believe this was her fellow snowshoer.

She flung snow to each side, her muscles burning. Digging as if her life depended on it, only it was *his* life instead.

Dizziness claimed her; she needed to rest, to take some deep breaths, but any pause could condemn him to death. *If it's him.*

The shovel scraped across dark green. Her heart expanded in relief. She threw herself onto her stomach and scooped snow out of the hole with her hands. He wasn't moving, he wasn't moving… Oh, God, which way was his head? If she resumed using the shovel, she might hurt him.

She realized she was talking to him, or maybe pleading with him. *Be alive. Don't leave me alone out here*—even though fifteen minutes ago she hadn't minded being alone at all.

With what had to take massive effort, he wrenched himself upward and gave his head a shake that scattered snow every which way. He gasped for breath.

"Are you all right?" Ava asked. Begged. "Are you all right?"

He turned his head enough so that he could see her. Snow-frosted brown hair, glassy eyes, a day or two's growth of beard on a strong face. Frozen blood in his hair and down his cheekbone and jaw.

"*God.* How did you find me?" Before she could answer, he shook his head again. "I'm stuck. I can't feel my legs."

"I'll keep digging." She calculated. "At an angle so I don't hit you."

He watched with what she guessed was unusual and maybe worrisome passivity.

Something made her look over her shoulder and up to the ridge that reared above the river. If those men had seen the avalanche, they might be scrambling down even now to help.

Or…maybe not. Either way, she didn't see anything, and it would surely take them hours to a full day to get this far.

She dug as hard and fast as she could, until he grunted and she realized the blade of the shovel had scraped over his knee. Now that she could see how his body lay imprisoned, she was able to dig with more confidence. She wasn't even aware of the soreness in her shoulders and upper arms anymore, or of the sharper pain shooting down her spine.

The man groaned, planted one hand on the ice to the side of the hole and heaved upward, twisting as he came. Agony flashed across his face. His leg broke free, but it appeared the other one was still trapped.

"You're injured," she said. *Duh*. How could he not be?

"Just get me out," he said from between clenched teeth.

Ava glared at him. "I'm doing my best."

His eyes closed. His voice became grittier. "I know you are."

Okay, foolish to take offense.

Moments later, he was free. He half pushed, half rolled out of the hole. That was the moment when she realized with dismay that *his* pack was nowhere to be seen.

Looking uphill toward the rock, she did see

something she'd missed: the other snowshoe, lying on the surface as if he'd casually tossed it aside.

He lay on the uneven surface, his head bare, and shook. As cold as she'd been, now she was sweating, but what she could see of his face was bone white, and he'd clamped his teeth together in a grimace that she felt sure was to keep them from chattering.

"We have to get you warm," she said. Decided. He was way worse off than she was.

She surveyed their surroundings and made herself think. Finding a way to warm him came first, ahead even of assessing his injuries.

Get him off the avalanche path. Pray he was able to walk, even if he had to lean on her to do it. Find a place to set up the tent. Laid out her sleeping bag. Maybe both of them would fit in it. She knew she needed to lie still, evaluate *herself* for injuries, gather herself for whatever needed doing next.

For the moment, she left the probe and shovel both in the snow and pushed herself to her feet. Her pack… There it was. She slung it onto her back again, the weight almost buckling her knees.

"You have to get up," she said. "I'm going to crouch down and help you."

He moved his head in agreement and, with what she guessed took superhuman will, pushed himself to his hands—no, one hand, she saw, his left arm dangled—and knees. She immediately became more aware of his sheer size. It wasn't only that he had to be several inches over six feet tall, but that he was broad. Shoulders, chest, powerful thighs. All of which meant he'd outweigh her by a sizeable amount. Nonetheless, she tucked herself under the crook of his uninjured arm and said, "Okay, let's do it."

They fought their way upright. His weight had her wanting to crumple, but she kept lifting. "That's it," she encouraged. "Upsy daisy."

The man lurched to his feet and his eyes met hers. He bit out, "Now…what?" before clamping his jaws together again. Shudders rattled his entire body.

"Down, toward those trees. It looks…kind of flat. I have a tent we can set up."

As they staggered, one step at a time, she kept talking without really knowing what she was saying. It hardly mattered; she couldn't imagine he was taking any of it in. The shaking came in waves, receding, then gripping his body again. She tried to time it so they could pause. If he went down, she had to wonder if she'd be able to get him up again.

Finally—*thank you, God, finally!*—they clambered awkwardly off the bottom of the avalanche flow onto snowy ground that was almost flat. Under the protection of evergreens blocking some of the sky, the snow wasn't as deep here as in most places, or they might have foundered.

Ava looked around, her uneasy remembrance of those men on the ridge making her want to find someplace that was out of sight. Yes, there. Low cedar branches hid a shadowy space behind. She steered the man there, pushed aside scratchy branches and finally had to help him lower to a sitting position so she could take off her pack and locate the tent.

When she bought it last winter to replace her old one, she'd almost chosen a bright red one, but now was glad she hadn't. She'd gone with dark green so it didn't stand out in a wild place, where she tried to pass as close to unseen as possible. Seeing that *her* hands were shaking now, too, she still unrolled a tarp and set out the tent. It was the kind that sprang up almost on its own. She also had a pad and sleeping bag that she unzipped.

"We need to take off your boots and some of your clothes," she told the stranger, who nodded jerkily but had to wait until she scooted close enough to untie his boots and yank them off, hoping she wasn't damaging an already injured knee or something like that. Gloves— they were really lucky his had stayed on, since he'd never have gotten those big hands into hers, even assuming she wasn't already wearing her backup ones. The glove had protected a watch, too. No hat to remove; that was gone. She unzipped his parka, the same color as her tent, and laid it atop the sleeping bag for some extra warmth.

Then she eyed the ice clinging to his snow pants and said, "I think these had better come off, too. I'll put them between the pad and sleeping bag and maybe they'll warm up and the ice will melt."

His expression showed no comprehension, but finally he looked down and nodded. With his one hand he unsnapped the waist but couldn't handle the zipper. Desperate to get them both warm—her sweat was making her feel colder by the second as it dried—Ava had lost all sense of personal boundaries. She unzipped his pants and, with another effort on his part, got him onto his one hand and knees again so she could peel the pants down and urge him to hop/crawl inside the tiny tent. She shoved the pants under the sleeping bag and helped him, wearing long underwear and a fleece top, scoot the rest of the way into the unzipped sleeping bag.

Aching to climb in after him, she listened to the uneasy voice in her head and made herself find a broken branch, which she used like a broom to brush away any clear signs of their trek from the edge of the ice-bound avalanche flow to their hidden refuge. Since they hadn't been able to go any distance, finding them wouldn't be hard, but…she'd done her best.

Only then did she take off her own gloves, boots, stretchy pants and quilted parka, and remove her fleece hat to pull it over his head before she lay down beside the big man who seemed worrisomely helpless.

Her parka she bunched to create an initially cold pillow. Zipping up the sleeping bag wasn't easy. She had to practically climb atop him to manage, then found herself pressed tightly against that long, hard, terrifyingly rigid body.

At last, at last, she burrowed her face into the crook between his neck and shoulder, let herself rest for a moment, then slipped her hands up under his fleece top and the waffle weave one that was beneath it. She began to rub his muscled torso with wide, sweeping movements.

"Warm," he mumbled, before he arched in another spasm of the shakes.

Since *she* didn't feel in the least warm, she was even more frightened by how cold he must be.

ZACH HAD BEEN seriously wounded twice in his army career, and he didn't think he'd ever felt as all-around terrible as he did right now. Still, hints of warmth began to penetrate; her heat must have lingered in the hat, and her breath on the bare skin of his neck felt like nirvana.

She was finding a lot of places that hurt as she moved her hands over his torso, but those hands felt deliciously hot, too, and he craved them. Higher, higher, he'd think, then lower. She didn't go quite as low as he really wanted, and he had a moment of wry humor. If he could convince her that was a top-notch way to warm him up... Yeah, probably not.

If he could even imagine getting horny or laughing again, he was probably going to survive, Zach decided.

"You hurt?" he managed to mumble.

Her hands paused. "I...don't really know," she said, sounding perplexed.

He understood. His head felt like a jackhammer had mistaken it for pavement that needed to be broken up. He knew something was very wrong with his shoulder, but otherwise…everything bloody hurt, so how could he identify any particular complaints? Once he was warm again, he decided.

"Your shoulder, or is it your arm…?" the woman said tentatively.

"Shoulder. Dislocated, I think." His damn teeth clattered every time he relaxed his jaw enough to speak. Given the spasms that shook the rest of him, the muscles surrounding his shoulder would be doing the same. Not good.

With a tremor in her voice, she asked, "Do you know how we can put it back into the socket?"

"Hope so, but… I need to get warm first." A vague memory suggested he had the order wrong—there was some reason the reduction should be done immediately—but he couldn't hold on to it.

"Okay." She snuggled closer, if that was possible.

He was able to press his cheek against her head, even though his stubble was probably going to tangle her disordered hair. It felt silky, though, and he'd seen some spilling out from beneath her hat when she was digging him out of the ice and snow. *Chestnut*, he thought was the right word. Her driver's license probably described her hair as brown, a lighter shade than his, but mixed in was a hint of something warmer. Red, he thought. It felt thick, warm. He wished he could bury his whole face in that tumble of hair, but suspected that wasn't logistically possible.

The movement of her hands slowed. Zach tried to zip his head so he could see her face, but their position made it almost impossible. Her rate of breathing dropped, too. She was falling asleep, he realized. Stress and exhaustion did often lead to a crash. He lifted his good arm enough to wrap it around her, securing her to his side. One of her hands slipped from beneath his shirt and she curled it next to her body, but the other remained splayed on his belly. Warm, comforting. He closed his eyes and wished he could zone out, too, but pain wouldn't allow him to surrender to unconsciousness.

He worried for a few minutes. What if he had internal bleeding? What if *she* did? More than most, he knew people could achieve heroics despite catastrophic injuries. Given how slender she was, the very fact that she'd dug him out quickly enough to save his life was astonishing.

Hell, finding him in the first place was downright miraculous.

Let her sleep, he told himself. *Pay attention*

in case she starts to struggle to breathe. He couldn't watch her, not as dim as the light was in the tent, nestled beneath heavy evergreen branches, not to mention how tightly the two of them were squeezed in here. As long as her breathing stayed even, she was okay.

Reality was, he might not be able to do anything to help if she did have a crisis.

Closing his eyes, shutting out the helplessness, he focused on her breathing alone. In, out. The tiny puff of air against his neck. The regularity reassured him, but also freed his mind to wander.

Automatic rifle. Worse, an RPG. Backcountry hikers in the US of A did not carry grenade launchers. He'd blanked both of those memories out since finding himself buried in what could have been an icy grave.

How *could* he have forgotten? Would those bastards be on their way to be sure they had successfully buried the witnesses? Or witness, singular, if they hadn't seen Zach?

Didn't matter; if they made it here, and he guessed anything like a straight line would be impossible, they'd see the huge hole the woman had dug to free him. Had she left any possessions there when she helped him down? Again, did that matter? The hole spoke for itself.

That she'd retained her pack was a miracle

itself. Not so much if she'd evaded the ava-lanche flow in the first place, but he guessed that wasn't the case or she wouldn't have sounded doubtful about whether she was hurt. Did she realize those men had deliberately trig-gered the avalanche?

Zach wondered, though. He hadn't been all there while she was setting up the tent, but she'd chosen an inconspicuous spot. By chance, because it was a level place she could find? Or because she was trying to tuck them out of sight?

Yeah, his mind wouldn't let up now that worries gathered, and he dealt with the unusual circumstance of not being able to do a damn thing to protect them. He'd curse the fact that he was unarmed because weapons were for-bidden in the national park, except his Glock would have been in a pocket in his backpack. The one that could be anywhere beneath the snow and ice.

If at all possible, he needed to go back out onto the avalanche to try to find his pack and snowshoes. He could only hope she'd found her own. They were in trouble if their mobil-ity was that severely limited.

And, hell, did she have enough food in her pack to feed both of them? For how many days? He presumed she at least had a phone that would give them hope of contacting the outside world when or if they emerged from this deep cut between a mountain and a high ridge, but that might be days away. The sat radio he'd carried, on loan from the border patrol, made finding his pack even more essential.

He realized his body had become rigid with tension. Not helping. Focus on her even breathing, the comfort of her supple, female body clasped to his, the lifesaving fact that she did have her pack with a tent, sleeping bag and at least minimal supplies. Without those, he'd be dead, and she wouldn't have had much hope.

Be damn grateful she was so gutsy.

AVA GRADUALLY SURFACED to realize that she must have fallen asleep. That was strange! She never napped, and now to drop off like a baby while she was squeezed into a sleeping bag with a strange man who'd scared her when she first realized he was chasing her down…

Fear tripped down her spine. No, she couldn't have left him to die. That had never been an option. But…now what?

Her body had obviously needed to take a time-out. She extended her senses to feel the entire length of his body, pressed against hers. He hadn't hurt her. He cradled her with one powerful arm. Her hand rested on his bare flesh, beneath his shirt. Right over his heartbeat, she realized, disconcerted. She felt the steady beat along with the tickle of chest hair.

Was *he* asleep? Instinct said no. There was too much tension in that body, and his breathing wasn't slow enough.

Ava cleared her throat. "Are you awake?"

He moved his head. "Yeah. How are you?"

That was a really good question. "Bruised all over," she decided, "and my back hurts, but more like I wrenched it than anything." She wriggled her toes. "Basically okay, I think."

"Good." There was a long pause. "'Upsy daisy'?"

"What?" Were her cheeks heating? "I don't know where I picked that up."

A vibration beneath her hand, breasts and cheek suggested a chuckle.

After a moment, she said, "I feel like I should get up. Except—"

When she broke off, his arm tightened. "We need to talk about what happened, and what we need to do to get out of this alive. We may as well be warm while we do that."

"I need to see your face."

After a pause, his arm relaxed. "Okay."

She squirmed until she could reach the zipper, then pulled it down enough to permit her to escape. Shivering, she took her parka from beneath his head and put it on.

He hadn't moved. Crossing her legs, she looked down at him. Then she swallowed and said, "Who are you? And…why were you following me?"

Chapter Three

"I've been asking myself who the hell *you* are and what you're doing out here on your own," he said with deceptive mildness, "but I don't mind starting. My name is Zach—Zachary— Reeves. I'm on vacation. I had a chance at a helicopter drop so I could enjoy some solitude in the wilderness." He wouldn't tell her yet that his ride had been courtesy of the US Border Patrol. "I was surprised to find out I wasn't alone, after all."

Yeah, that was suspicion in her eyes. Eyes that appeared dark in this light, but he suspected were blue. Bruises discolored one of her cheekbones and her forehead on the same side, but under other circumstances she'd be a beautiful woman, he realized for the first time.

"We must have chosen the same route," he continued. "I came across your tracks yesterday and…" He hesitated, then moved one shoulder. Even that sent a stab of agony through the other, although he was more disturbed by the numbness in his arm. "Was curious, I guess. I was faster than you, so I gained ground."

"Vacation," she said flatly. "Most people go to Honolulu in the winter."

"What are *you* doing here? This backcountry is closed for another couple of months."

"I'm a wildlife photographer. One of the magazines I sell to pulled some strings, and park officials dropped me off and arranged to pick me up again…um, three days from now?" She frowned. "I think. My name is Ava Brevick."

Wasn't familiar to him, but he couldn't remember ever glancing at the photographer's name when he did see photographs of wildlife, however spectacular.

"Well, we have some big problems now," he said bluntly.

Her eyebrows rose. "You think?"

"How did you find your pack?"

"It was still on my back." She reached over to lift at some loose nylon fabric. "I had an airbag, and just long enough before the avalanche hit me to pull on the cord to activate it. It's supposed to help keep you on top, and in this instance it worked."

"What about your snowshoes? Your poles?"

He hadn't noticed her camera and asked about that, too.

"My poles and snowshoes are long gone. My camera strap held. In fact, it tried to strangle me." She pulled down her turtleneck to reveal ugly bruises that made it look like she'd been garroted. Carefully covering her neck again, she said, "I did find your snowshoes. They didn't look damaged. I guess I left them out there, but they'll be easy to find."

"Poles?"

Shaken head.

"Maybe if we poke around, we can find my pack."

"We can try," she said doubtfully.

He gave a slight nod to acknowledge her pessimism. Or call it realism. He'd hold off explaining why recovering his pack was so critical.

"You know we didn't set off that avalanche."

She frowned. "You're saying it was just chance that it went while we were in the way?"

"No. Those men you were watching up on the ridge," he said bluntly. "Did you notice the weapons they were carrying?"

"Yes." It was almost a whisper, and she blanched. "I think they saw me. I noticed sun reflecting off glass. It almost had to be the lens of binoculars."

Or the scope on a high-powered rifle. But he didn't say that.

"Probably. They didn't expect to encounter anyone out here. I'm reasonably sure they sneaked across the Canadian border."

The woman—Ava—nodded. "That's what I thought, too. It was so weird seeing anyone up there. A wildfire must have opened up the top of the ridge. Even so, it has to be really difficult terrain."

"They used something like an RPG—a grenade launcher—to set off the avalanche. Whatever they fired was visible crossing the sky. Pretty sure they fired a second one, too, just to be sure. I don't know if they noticed me. Either way, they thought they'd take care of any witnesses."

Ava stared at him for a minute, making him think of an owl blinking in bemusement. "I… almost forgot about them."

"I did, too. We've had more pressing issues."

"Oh, God. You don't think—"

"I don't know," he admitted. "It was smart of you to set up the tent out of sight."

"I was glad it wasn't red."

He tipped his head, but decided not to ask about that.

"And…after you got in the sleeping bag, I went back out and used a broken branch to smooth away our tracks." She made a face. "More or less. So I guess I didn't completely forget them."

"You were smart," he said approvingly. He wished she hadn't left his snowshoes behind, but did that matter? Little as he liked the idea of either of them spending time in the open, he had to search for his pack.

She gave herself a shake. "You're hurt worse than I am. I should take a look…" In fact, she reached into her pack and pulled out some sterile wipes.

"Like I said, I think my shoulder is dislocated." He hoped that was what was wrong. A dislocation was fixable; shattered bones weren't under the circumstances. Shattered bones might have done nerve damage that would explain the numbness and the weird tingling he felt in his fingertips. If that were so, even if he made it to a hospital, he might have done too much damage for surgical repair to be possible. Even though it was on his weak side, the injury had the potential to end his newfound career.

He held still while she used one of the wipes on his face. Stinging told him there were cuts and scrapes, at the least, but she sat back, looking satisfied. "Anything besides the shoulder?" she asked.

He had one hell of a headache, but why tell her? He'd probably suffered a concussion. There'd been a few moments of double vision, and he was currently nauseated. None of that meant he could afford to lie around waiting to feel better.

"Bruises, like you," he said. "Maybe a cracked rib or two."

"You said you thought we could put your arm back in the socket." The idea clearly made her feel queasy, and he didn't blame her given that she wasn't a medical professional.

The hot coal of pain in his shoulder was making it hard to think, and would surely prevent him doing anything else, though. "I was…a soldier. I've done it for other people a couple of times." And no, he hadn't loved the experience, even though he'd had some medic training. "It works better if you have an assistant, but as it is…"

She took a deep, visible breath and gave a choppy nod. "I'll do whatever I have to do."

His admiration for Ava became something else he didn't let himself examine.

HE ADMITTED THAT they should have done this much sooner, that muscle spasms could prevent the bone from being manipulated back into the socket. He'd *known* that, but in his misery, had pushed the knowledge back.

"On the other hand, I guess you could say we iced it."

Ava gave a small, choked laugh that made his lips twitch.

Hey, he'd have been screwed if he'd been alone, as he'd expected to be.

"Might be easier if I weren't wearing anything, but I'm not about to try to wrestle my shirt off."

"And we can't cut it off, given that none of my clothes would fit you."

"Yeah." He described accomplishing a reduction of a shoulder dislocation as well as he could, keeping it simple. Ideally, he should sit up at about a thirty-degree angle. Maybe they could manage that if she propped her pack behind him. She would have to gently pull, applying traction while also rotating the arm outward until she felt the pop of the ball going back into the socket. It would help if he wasn't screaming. "If there's too much swelling or the muscles object too violently, it might not work."

"Then we'll pack your shoulder with snow and try again later," she said sturdily.

She was quite a woman, he thought again, even as he couldn't help also noticing the delicacy of her bone structure and the firmness of a chin that some would call stubborn. Stubborn was fine by him.

"I wish…" she began, before falling silent.

"You wish?"

"That there was someone else to hold you in place."

That would be ideal, but he'd do what he had to. He blinked against sweat dripping into his eyes. The pain was getting to him. He wanted to get this over with.

"I'm going to bite down on something to keep myself from yelling. Don't want to draw attention."

Her head bobbed. Her eyes were huge as she maneuvered in the small space, inevitably bumping into him a few times and making him wince, to wedge her pack behind him and punch it into a shape that let him half recline.

"Okay?"

"Yeah," he said hoarsely.

Now she half crawled until she was beside him on his bad side, forced to bend over by the curving roof of the small tent.

"One hand here." She gripped his upper arm. "The other on your wrist."

"Yeah. You might want to move down a little so you can pull harder."

She nodded and adjusted her position.

He'd begun to feel like someone waiting for the executioner to do his thing. If this didn't work—if something else altogether was wrong with his shoulder—would he be able to do his part getting them out of this remote country before they starved, froze…or were cornered by men he guessed were terrorists?

Too well armed for mere smugglers, anyway.

I CAN DO THIS.

Ava repeated the few words as if they were a mantra. Except, wasn't that the concept she already lived by? After years of having next to no control over where she went or how she lived, she'd dedicated herself to changing that. She'd made a success of a career defined by independence. If she could do that, she could do a little thing like this.

She gulped, took a deep breath and began applying pressure, pulling an arm that was easily twice as thick as hers, so muscular that, uninjured, he could probably pick her up with just that arm and toss her over his head.

His back arched. Tendons stood out in his neck, and he bared his teeth around the clean sock she'd offered for him to clench. She didn't dare look into his dark brown eyes, but she knew they'd dilated and never left her face.

Continuing pressure. Rotate outward. You can do this.

It seemed an eternity before she felt and even thought she heard the pop. Ava almost let out a whimper and slumped, but instead followed the remainder of his instructions and gently rotated the arm back toward his body, bent it at the elbow and laid his forearm across his torso.

He shuddered, spit out the sock and swore a few times, creatively.

"Thank God," he finally mumbled.

"It worked." She really hadn't expected it would, Ava was ashamed to realize. Something like that should have been done in a hospital ER, or at the very least by experienced paramedics.

"Yeah." His throat worked. "Pain let up."

"It…can't possibly be fixed that easily."

He grunted. "No. I should wear a sling, but maybe we can figure out how to brace the shoulder. We can't just sit here and wait for rescue."

No. They couldn't.

"You don't have poles, anyway," she pointed out.

"We can make some out of sticks." He frowned, reaching with his good hand to knead the injured shoulder. "If I had my pack, I could jury-rig snowshoes for you. Any chance you carry some cord I could use to tie branches together?"

"I do. It seemed like it might come in handy."

"Good girl." His grin changed a face that had so far seemed grim into one that was both warm and sexy.

"What do you do for a living?" she heard herself ask. Why hadn't it occurred to her to wonder before?

His expression returned to impassive. "I'm a cop."

"A cop." Did she believe him? She wondered again about the chance of him appearing at the same time as those men on the ridge.

"Whatcom County, the northwest corner of the state. Other side of Mount Baker. I'm a detective." He hesitated, watching her. "I got out of the service a year ago. Adjustment to a civilian life isn't as easy as you'd think."

"I've never thought about it." She pushed herself up to an awkward, bent-over position and clambered over his legs. "It's still light. I think I'll go grab everything I left out there. Maybe…maybe I should kind of fill in the hole."

"You're not going alone." He sat up.

"Yes, I am." She hoped he heard the steel in her voice. "If those men show up, they'd just grab you, too. You're not armed." As far as she knew. "If you won't rest *for even a few minutes*—" she leaned hard on that "—you could scout around for some branches that might work to make me snowshoes. I have a pocket-knife you can use to cut the branches."

He didn't seem to like her being the one to put herself out there and argued against it, but he had to know she was right. Even if the men who'd triggered the avalanche had continued on their route along the ridge, putting from their mind the two people they'd gone out of their way to bury in snow and ice, Ava and Zach would have a difficult trek out of here with such limited supplies. They had to plan to leave first thing in the morning, and keep moving to the extent of their physical ability. Even fully equipped and in peak condition, they would be looking at a minimum of two to three more nights spent along the way. Now—

They would do the best they could.

"I'm not talking convenience, here," he said, voice clipped. "I have a satellite radio in that pack. We need to be able to call for help, and your phone isn't going to cut it."

He talked some more, although he'd already convinced her. The idea that he might be able to call for help *right this minute*—although she hadn't thought to ask if the thing had any limitations—was compelling.

She did win the argument about who would be going out to search, though. Dressed again, Ava felt like a mouse creeping out of hiding, excruciatingly aware that the cat might be watching her every timid move.

SHE MUST HAVE napped for a surprising length of time as they'd struggled to recover from the avalanche, because the light was already going, and fast. Days were still short in the Pacific Northwest at this time of year, and they were a lot shorter with mountains shadowing the valleys cut deep by rivers formed from glacial runoff.

It didn't take Ava long to return to the gaping hole that could well have been Zach Reeves's grave. Lovely thought. She stood still for a long moment, looking around, listening, but neither saw nor heard any evidence that other human beings were in the vicinity. Apprehension stuck with her, though—crawling up the back of her neck.

She seized the probe first, and began stabbing it into the much hardened avalanche flow, starting below where she'd found him, then working her way uphill from where he'd ended up. Nothing. She hit hard objects over and over again, but when she uncovered them, all she found were blocks of ice or rocks. Finally, she grabbed his snowshoes, then debated climbing up to see if there was any chance she'd missed seeing her own.

A shiver crawled over her, reminding her how exposed she was, how easily someone from quite a distance away could see her. Say, someone descending the ridge behind her.

Exhaustion already had her shaking. Rested, she could try again in the morning to find his pack. He'd convinced her that radio could be their salvation, and she was scared enough to believe him.

Finally she picked up the shovel and started scraping the snow and chunks of ice she'd dug out of the hole back into it. Her muscles burned and her back protested, but she kept at it until…well, she hadn't one hundred percent disguised the hole, but given how uneven the surface of a fresh avalanche flow was, it probably wasn't visible from very far away.

Zach, she suspected, would have searched longer and harder for his pack, the contents of which would come in really handy above and beyond the radio, but she'd reached her limit. She might have to sit on him to keep him from coming out here to poke and poke in a widening semicircle as darkness fell, but so be it.

She might have to sit on him to keep him from doing it, anyway.

Not that sitting on him would have much effect, she feared; he'd probably just pick her up and set her aside like a toddler who'd gotten in his way. Except that he'd damn well better not try anything like that, given the stomach-turning unpleasantness of...what had he called it? *Reduction of a dislocated shoulder.* That was it. And she did not want to repeat it, even assuming it would work a second time, because he was too foolish to recognize that, however temporarily, he had limitations.

Once again, she found a branch she used to brush away her footprints as well as she could, discarding it once she pushed between the feathery limbs of the cedar tree. Zach sat cross-legged in the doorway of her tent, head up as he watched her approach. His gaze swept over her from head to toe, taking in the few items she carried.

He'd found a way to halfway support his left arm using a cotton turtleneck from her pack. The gloved hand emerging from his minimal sling gripped a long branch he was stripping of smaller offshoots with the blade of her pocketknife. He had a fair pile of similar branches lying in front of him.

"You think that will work?" she asked doubtfully.

"In theory. I take it you didn't find the pack."

"No." She dropped the snowshoes at his side and thrust the shovel into the crusty snow, then folded the probe so she could stow it in her pack again.

He continued to study her with those penetrating dark eyes. "You have to hurt more than you're letting on. And be in shock."

"I'm not—"

Ignoring her protest, he said, "Come closer so I can measure the length of these against you."

After he'd learned whatever it was he needed to know, he muttered, "I hate to start cutting up the cord. If I screw up, we can't tie it back together."

She moved over so she could get into the tent and sat with a groan she hoped he didn't hear. His broad back blocked much of the light as she poked around in her pack.

"I have a stove. I could heat up a meal," she offered.

He turned. "How many meals do you have left?"

Counting was what she'd just been doing. "Um…five." And that only because she'd brought two or three extras, just in case.

"Then I'm going to say no. If you have any snacks, let's stick to those. I had an adequate meal last night, and I'm guessing you did, too."

Ava nodded.

"Worse comes to worst, I can try my hand at trapping rabbits or other small mammals, but that would mean starting a real fire, and until we're sure we're alone, I don't want to do that."

Her head bobbed again. She *wanted* to argue, but couldn't reasonably do so. Her stomach was growling, but she wouldn't starve in the next day. A handful of almonds would suffice.

Zach had already gone back to work, only saying over his shoulder, "See if you can find something that might work as a strap across the front of your boots."

Oh, lord. There had to be something.

"My camera strap," she started to say before changing her mind.

But he turned again, his suddenly intense gaze boring into hers. "You watched those men. Did you get any photos of them?"

She couldn't look away from him. "I…yes. But…what difference does that make? It's not as if either of us would *know* any of them."

"If you got their faces, there's one guy I might recognize. He's on a watch list I just saw."

He'd seen a watch list because he was a cop?

Her thoughts took a jump. "You're border patrol."

He shook his head. "No, I told you. I have a friend who is, though. We served together. He's the one who gave me the lift out here. There have been rumors about an assassin whose bomb making is notable, too, available for hire to select fanatic causes, who rumor also says is on his way to the US. You know, the northern border of the US is considered the longest undefended border in the world. It's something like fifty-five hundred miles. Patrols are spread so far apart on the wilderness stretches with no roads, my buddy asked me to keep an eye out, even though the chances of me seeing anything were next to nothing."

"What would he look like, this assassin?"

"He's Russian."

Caucasian, as all the men had appeared to be. Shaken, she fumbled for her camera. "I can show you what I did get."

What if…?

Chapter Four

Zach wouldn't have been surprised if Ava found her camera to be irreparably damaged. The lens showed definite damage. But he held his breath as she lifted the camera and did her thing. An image showed on the screen, although he was too far away to make out more detail than to know he was looking at a snowshoe hare. That didn't mean she'd captured a face clear enough to identify from such a distance, but he couldn't drag his gaze away from the images that continued to whisk by.

Then there was one, a figure clad in white that stood out against the intensely blue sky. A man.

"You mind?" he asked, and when she shook her head, he maneuvered himself closer to her. He ignored the jab of pain trying to persuade him to stay still. Tough. Blocking pain was nothing new to him; he could do it again. He was already ignoring the fact that his skull was splitting open.

Maybe literally fractured? He couldn't let himself think about that.

He studied the digital photo in amazement. There was no visible face; the guy was wearing a balaclava, at a guess, but small as the figure was, the image was still sharp enough he could see quilted pants, heavy boots—and the weapon slung across the man's shoulder.

Ava glanced at Zach, and he nodded. Two pictures later, one of the men had his face uncovered. It was almost in profile. Thin, tanned face. After close study, he shook his head, and she moved on. Two more wearing balaclavas, and then came a man looking directly toward the camera.

Zach hissed in a breath. Ava turned her head and, wide-eyed, stared at him.

"That's him. I'm almost positive. Those cheekbones are unusual. Jaw broader than usual, too. You can't see his widow's peak, but—" He broke off. "Grigor Borisyuk has only been caught by a camera once that the US government knows about. It was a news photographer who took the photo. He was strongly advised to transfer to a domestic beat after that."

"Did he?"

"My friend didn't say. He'd have been foolish not to." Although foreign news correspondents and photographers were known more for guts than common sense.

There was no saying Borisyuk would have bothered hunting down the photographer, of course; once the picture was out there, what was the point? He was known to be ruthless and utterly lacking a conscience, though, according to Reid. Zach didn't imagine Borisyuk as the sort of fellow who'd shrug and say, "Ah, well."

And now a second photographer had recorded his face, with him staring straight at her. He might not have known she held a camera, but someone in their party had seen her through binoculars, which increased the odds that it was Borisyuk who had snapped out an order to kill the observer.

Zach's instinct screamed: pack up *now* and get the hell out of here.

If only it was possible. They weren't going anywhere until he finished the crude snowshoes he was constructing and they found sturdy sticks suitable to serve as poles, by which time it would be dark.

The sky had deepened; the change subtle enough he hadn't noticed. He had to get back to work. They wouldn't want to show a light, that was for sure.

"Straps to hold your boots?" he asked, scooting back to where he'd set down the peculiar bunch of branches. He still had some cord, but less than he'd like.

"Oh, ah…" Looking shaken, Ava didn't move for a minute. Then, "We can cut pieces off the straps on the pack." She twisted and turned her backpack so he could see the tough compression straps used to lessen the bulk of the load, as well as straps dangling after she'd adjusted the fit for her relatively small body.

"Perfect," he declared.

She held out her booted foot for him to measure the lengths he'd need, then watched as he used the pocketknife to cut several lengths. Then, little as he liked it, she left to hunt for straight, solid sticks long enough to serve as poles for both of them.

Her absence split his attention, but he made himself keep working. Right now, she was fitter than he was, smart and capable. A protective instinct had kicked in the minute he saw the avalanche begin its roaring descent toward her, but he had to rein it in. The only way to get out of here was to trust each other.

Turned out she had a small folding saw in her pack, which she took with her. He couldn't believe the crowd from the ridge were near enough to hear even if he and she burst into song, but he was just as glad she didn't have to snap off any branches she found, even if that recognizable cracking sound was common in the backcountry when heavy snow weighted tree limbs down.

She came back sooner than he'd expected, and presented four only slightly curved or crooked sticks that looked sturdy and which she'd stripped of any growth.

"Those look good," he said with a nod.

He saw a flicker of something in her eyes at his approval—humor?—but then she sat down just inside the tent with a sigh. Pulling her pack to her, she rooted around and handed him a small packet of mixed nuts and a box of raisins, the kind his mom had put in his school lunch when he was a kid.

The mother whose face he had trouble recalling, given how long ago she'd died.

Ava produced a water bottle and they both took sips, Zach accepting another couple of ibuprofen. He thought about suggesting she use her stove to boil water, but the bottle was the only one they had, and it was still three-quarters full. Wait until midday or later tomorrow, he decided. They didn't dare let themselves get dehydrated.

Unsure if his unsettled stomach would accept anything he sent its way, he ate the nuts and raisins anyway, before taking another couple of sips of water, as did she. Then they moved out of the tent so she could try the crude snowshoes. He had to make several adjustments and still wasn't convinced the bootstraps would hold.

"Take a few steps," he said. "Better lift your feet higher than usual."

She did and looked down in surprise. "They're heavier than my snowshoes were, but…it works."

"Green wood," he told her. "I hope we don't have to break into a run. This isn't the most solid construction ever, but in theory it should work." He glanced around. "Damn, it's getting dark."

"It happens fast here."

"I know." He shoved himself to his feet. "I need to, ah, use the facilities, then let's try to sleep as soon as possible. I want to go back out there to try to find my pack—" even though the chances lessened as the avalanche flow hardened "—and that'll have to be at first light. We can't afford to take long."

Despite what had to be fear on her fine-boned face, this nod was as sturdy as all her previous agreements had been. He'd prefer to have an army teammate as backup, someone with serious muscle who also happened to have a weapon secreted in his backpack, but—otherwise?—Zach was astonished at how lucky he'd gotten that the woman who had catapulted them into this by taking a few photos was also gutsy, strong and determined.

Now, if only they could escape and contact the people who needed to see that photograph before Grigor Borisyuk succeeded at disappearing into the American population.

"WE'LL NEED TO sleep together," Ava said as matter-of-factly as she could manage. Why she'd felt compelled to say that, she didn't know. What else were they supposed to do? It just...felt like the elephant in the room. Well, the tent. "I hope we *can* sleep so squished together," she added. Although she'd already proved to herself that she could. Ava suspected he hadn't dropped off at all earlier, though.

With the increasingly murky light, she couldn't make out Zach's features any better than he presumably could hers. Lucky, since she suspected she was blushing.

And how ridiculous was that? She hadn't hesitated to wedge herself into that sleeping bag with him when the necessity had been so dire. Well, it still was. To survive, they had to sleep, and they had to share. *So get over it*, she told herself.

"We've had practice," he said drily, his deep voice having more impact after the darkness had shuttered her vision.

She pushed aside the sleeping bag and laid her outer layer of clothing onto the too-thin pad. From rustling sounds, movement and a grunt that was likely pain, Zach was stripping, as well. A moment later, he handed her his garments and she laid them out, too.

Then she shook out the sleeping bag atop the clothing and pad.

"Um…are we more likely to bump your arm if you get in first, or if I do?" she asked.

"I'd better go first. I can't prop myself up very well, and given our respective weights, I should be on the bottom, anyway."

Well, that was true enough, and he'd certainly been tactful. "Respective weights" indeed. He surely out-weighed her by eighty pounds, and perhaps as much as a hundred.

So she waited while he lay down, shifted a few times, then said, "Okay."

Ava zipped up the bag more than halfway before squirming until she was far enough in to rest her head on his chest. Then she groped for the zipper and pulled it up, excruciatingly aware of his contours.

Pretend he's a body pillow, she told herself. *Don't think of him as a man with big bones and powerful muscles.* Especially *don't think of him as the stranger he is.*

The stranger she had no choice but to trust.

She did her very best to lie still, even though one arm was bent awkwardly beneath her and she couldn't quite figure out what to do with the other one.

He shifted and wrapped *his* arm around her. "Try to get comfortable," he ordered.

She rolled her eyes, but wriggled until her position was the best she could manage. She hoped she hadn't hurt him. Then she sighed.

"I'm not very sleepy," she said after a moment. "It's early, and... I took a nap."

His chest vibrated in what she took as a laugh. "So you did. You needed it."

"Yes. It's just..." How to put into words how shaken she was by all the shocks, slamming one atop another? They tumbled through her head: the anxiety awakened by her awareness that she was no longer alone, was possibly even being pursued; the peculiar and then worrying sight of armed men where they shouldn't have been; the terror of being caught in an avalanche, followed by the possibly greater terror of thinking she wouldn't be able to find and dig out the other person caught in it. Never mind squeezing into the sleeping bag with the stranger who'd scared her, the icky task of manipulating his arm back into the socket—she still shivered, thinking about it—and finally the horrifying discovery that she may have photographed a terrorist sought throughout the free world. A terrorist who could only be sneaking into the US for a purpose that chilled her blood.

"I understand," he said quietly, his breath stirring her hair. His arm tightened slightly around her. "I'm…used to combat, but I don't love the night before I know there'll be action."

She tried to lift her head and failed. "You think there will be tomorrow?"

The pause felt longer than it probably was. "I hope not. I won't lie, though. If that is Borisyuk, he has damn good reason to want to ensure no witnesses are able to report his arrival in this country. That said—" the hand that had been tucked around her torso made a movement that might have been a waggle "—from their perspective, odds are good the avalanche took you out."

"Could they have seen that I pulled myself out?"

"I doubt it. From what you said, you were carried way down the slope. Both of us were. Tree cover is heavy along the creek."

She let herself relax a tiny bit, her mind wandering as she considered how intimate this felt, talking quietly in the night while wrapped in each other's arms. Not something she'd had in a very long time.

"The smartest thing they could do is go on their way," he continued. "Even if you survived, even if they had a glimpse of me, any experience at all would tell them how likely it was that if one or the other of us survived, we'd have been injured, and we'd be hindered by losing some of our equipment. If they got well ahead of us, they can tuck Borisyuk into whatever bolt-hole was planned, and assume we couldn't identify any of them. In fact, even seeing your camera, why would they think you'd have actually gotten a photo of him?"

She appreciated his reassurance, but couldn't take it at face value.

"You think that's what will happen, then? They'll go on?"

Another pause had her stiffening. "I don't know," he admitted. "The guy hasn't been so successful, moving like a ghost until he completes his job, then disappearing again, if he isn't ultracareful. Paranoid."

Her mouth suddenly dry, she swallowed against a swell of panic. "We should be—"

He gave her a little shake. "You know we

can't travel in the dark. Even fully equipped, it would be foolish. As it is, a good snag will tear one of your snowshoes apart. I'm confident that they will have as difficult a time dropping down to the river valley, assuming that's what they're thinking of doing."

"They'd have to, at some point."

"Yes, but doesn't a trail drop down off the ridge farther south? It'll be buried under snow, but will still be more navigable than heading out cross-country."

She bobbed her head.

"I'm…not sure I like that option, either, though." He spoke more slowly. "It's fine if they drop down the west side of the ridge, but I don't like the idea of them popping out in front of us."

Don't like the idea. What a splendid euphemism for a squad of terrorists spreading a net to catch Zach and her.

And yet, the two of them had no options at all. They couldn't hunker down where they were and hope their nonappearance convinced the bad guys they were dead and buried under the avalanche, because they didn't have enough food to survive for more than a handful of days, plus they'd need to trek out to where they might have cell service. Her ride had been prearranged…but they'd never make it there in time, not inadequately equipped and injured as they were.

Also...while she had never so much as considered joining the armed forces, she didn't like the idea of she and Zach protecting themselves at the cost of their nation. They *had* to get the word out.

If he'd told her the truth about himself and his background, it occurred to her, he must be utterly determined to do whatever was required to stop an evil man from carrying his war of twisted ideals into their home country. Wasn't that what he'd dedicated his life to?

His concern for her had been evident so far, but however calming his deep voice was in the darkness, however comforting the hot length of his body and the solid shoulder beneath her cheek, saving her had to be second on his list of priorities. And, while she couldn't blame him for that, the realization was...frightening.

What could she say? Nothing came to her, and he remained silent, too, even though she knew that, for the longest time, he was no more asleep than she was.

HE MUST HAVE awakened at least hourly all night. At one point, he'd have gotten up to use the john, but the impracticality of that persuaded him to shove the mere thought to the back of his mind. They had to sleep while they could.

A part of him, sleeping and awake, was listening for any sound that didn't belong. He hated knowing the enemy carried fully automatic weapons while he didn't have so much as a handgun. If only he could get his hands on one of those rifles…

Could he use it, given his present disability? He tightened his fingers into a fist a few times without any noticeable increase in pain. Yeah, he thought he could. Certainly if it was life or death.

He made himself slow his breathing, courting sleep. How long it lasted, he didn't know, but this time when he opened his eyes, he was able to make out the peak of the tent above him. The light, if you could call it that, held barely a hint of gray, but it was enough.

He tipped his head toward Ava's ear. "Up and at 'em."

"Is that sort of like upsy daisy?" she mumbled.

He grinned. "Yeah."

She didn't move right away. "I *ache*."

Now that he thought about it, so did he, and it wasn't just his shoulder and head. Of course they hurt. They'd both been beaten within an inch of their lives yesterday. When he said so, she groaned.

"I haven't forgotten. Ugh."

"You can stay cozy for a little longer while I go poke around for my pack," he suggested.

She rolled her eyes. "Don't be silly. Just... give me a minute."

Her minute was brief enough, so he didn't have to push. She sighed and wriggled her way against his body until she was free of the warm sleeping bag. Zach couldn't help thinking he'd be aching in a different way if they didn't both hurt, and their situation wasn't so urgent.

"Brr!" she exclaimed. "Roll over!"

He obliged, and she snatched up first his clothes, thrusting them at him, before grabbing her own and scrambling into them.

His shoulder and arm had stiffened up during the night, not surprisingly, and getting his quarter-zip fleece top on was a challenge. By the time he succeeded, Ava had shoved her feet into her boots and was separating the flaps of the tent.

"Wait!" he said sharply.

"We're still alone." She slipped out, and he heard a hint of a footfall and then nothing.

Damn it! She probably had to pee—now that he'd thought about it, he was near to desperation himself—but he didn't like her taking the lead.

As if he could have protected her if a terrorist materialized in front of them, Zach thought, disgruntled at his own weakness and frustrated anew at being unarmed. He used his left hand to help him get his boots on, then half crawled, half hopped out of the tent before rising to his feet. Ava pushed aside a feathery, low-hanging cedar branch and stepped into sight.

"I'll dig out something for us to eat."

"Thanks." He went the same direction she had, relieved himself, then detoured for a glimpse at the avalanche flow. The light was brighter up above the peak; down here in the vee of the valley, details were still elusive. He wondered how firmly the ice and snow had set, whether it would even be possible to dig a hole in it now. Damn, he hoped the hole Ava Brevick *had* dug wasn't visible to eyes looking for just that.

She'd already rolled the sleeping bag when he returned but left the pad open for them to sit on as they quickly ate more nuts and some dried apricots. His queasiness lingered, but if he had to expel this small amount of food, it wouldn't take more than a minute, and he could hope to do it without her noticing. He chased the bites with a few swallows of extremely cold water. Worse came to worst, he reminded himself, they could drink from the river where it appeared between sheets of ice and snow. Becoming infected with a possible bacteria wouldn't kill them in the near future, although odds were good she carried tablets to purify water.

He was left feeling useless as he watched her roll the pad and dismantle the tent, stow the tent in her pack and finally strap the roll and sleeping bag together where they'd rest on her lower back.

"I'll carry that," he said.

She yanked it toward herself, her expression indignant. "Don't be ridiculous! You're *injured*."

Ready to argue, Zach opened his mouth, but she added, "Besides, I'd rather have you able to keep watch and…and respond or at least make decisions if you see or hear anything."

He glared at her, then let his head fall forward. Fine, but he had no weapon. How was he supposed to "respond"?

The very question pulled him back from the frustration that served no purpose. She was right—and he needed to start thinking about what he *could* turn into a weapon, or how, if the opportunity arose, he could take out one man—and acquire ample food, weapons and equipment for him *and* Ava.

"We'll talk about it again once we really get started," he said roughly. "Okay. You all set?"

There was the nod that caused a squeezing sensation under his breastbone every time he saw it. He thrust his feet into the snowshoe bindings, saw her do the same with her make-shift ones, and they both gripped their sturdy sticks.

He stepped out from the shelter provided by the cedar tree, took a good look around and started out over really difficult ground. This would be a test of her snowshoes.

It didn't take them five minutes to reach the foot of the avalanche flow, which he really took in for the first time. A hundred and fifty yards wide or more, he estimated, stunned. The sheer amount of material flung down the slope was frightening. It was a miracle they'd survived—particularly that she'd found him. Good God, what made him think there was a chance in hell of stumbling on his pack in the vastness of this avalanche field?

He had to try.

They tried, at the stubborn woman's insistence, but he weakened fast. A couple of times dizziness brought him to his knees. He waved off her concern, pretending he thought he'd spotted something.

It was a relief when the hour he'd given them for the search was up. Premature relief, given the day facing them. A short rest was all he allowed them. Increasing awareness of the sun rising and the enemy that might be in pursuit drove him to ignore his physical limitations.

Once they were on their feet, on their way, he just hoped Ava's snowshoes held up until they reached the trail they'd both traversed yesterday, where the way would become somewhat easier. Trail or no, though, they wouldn't be able to move fast enough to stay ahead of any serious pursuit.

Chapter Five

Ava fell down twice in the first twenty yards or so. The first time, she failed to notice a rock lurking just beneath the snow and crashed down with an *uumph*.

Zach swung around in alarm, but fortunately she'd come out of the snowshoes, which didn't appear damaged. She made a face at him, ignored what was sure to be a new and painful bruise on her hip, and levered herself back up with the help of her pole. Booted toes back under the straps, she started out again behind him.

The second time, a springy whip of alder or something equally bedeviling snagged her. Now, a couple of the more fragile crosspieces in one of the snowshoes snapped, but after Zach crouched and examined it, he said, "I think it's still solid enough."

He was kind enough not to add, *If you don't put too much stress on it*. But she'd known, as well as he must, that this stretch where there never had been a trail cut, never mind maintained, would be the hardest going. Next to impossible, if not for the snow cover that buried some of the rocks and teeming growth the river valleys in this temperate rainforest were known for.

Their pace felt, and undoubtedly was, glacially slow. He'd have been able to go way faster if he wasn't stuck with her, she thought, but then it wasn't her fault that her snowshoes had been lost in the avalanche. She more than made up for that handicap with the supplies in her pack she *had* held on to.

Between each stride, she held her breath, however fleetingly, so that she could listen for the sounds of anyone else moving behind them. Zach must have been doing the same.

Despite her own struggles, she became aware that he wasn't moving with the smooth efficiency she'd seen when she spotted the man gaining ground on her yesterday. Of course he wasn't! What if his arm popped out of the socket again?

She took a couple of hurried steps and said, "Are you all right?"

He stopped and turned at the waist to look at her. "What?"

"Your shoulder. What if you reinjure it?"

For a long moment, his expression didn't change. Then he grimaced, deepening lines she'd already seen on his face. Yes, he hurt.

"I'm wondering if we can strap my upper arm to my torso so that only my lower arm is free."

He must've hated having to keep admitting to any vulnerabilities, but he was doing it, anyway.

"It'll be hard for you to use your pole effectively, but… I don't see why not. Why don't you look for someplace we can at least set the pack down and maybe sit?"

"How are you doing?" he asked, his gaze holding hers.

What her body needed right this minute was a spa with hot bubbling water loosening painful muscles, but he must feel worse.

"Fresh as a daisy."

His grin took her breath away. "Like daisies, do you?"

"As a matter of fact, I do."

She soaked in the power of that smile and the glint of warmth and humor in his eyes until he inevitably turned away and started out again.

Two steps later, her right stick plunged into a hole. Leaning on it as she was, she stumbled, barely saving herself from falling to her knees.

Although she regained her balance, despair grabbed her. Even aside from possible pursuit—or an ambush set in front of them—how could they hope to cover enough miles with her walking sloppily on a bunch of small branches, and falling every ten minutes?

Zach must not have noticed her latest mishap, because twenty feet opened between them before she braced herself and resumed the clumsy, knees-high marching steps. What was she going to do? Drum her heels and whine, *I can't do this*? They had no choice at all. This was life and death, and not only for them.

I'm stronger than this, she told herself, and fixed her gaze on the man leading the way despite his own pain.

FOR THE NEXT ten or fifteen minutes, it was all Zach could do not to turn his head constantly to check on Ava. He didn't like the fact that she was both the one to have to struggle with the jury-rigged snowshoes and to carry a heavy pack while he strode ahead unhindered.

He'd have suggested he try to convert his snowshoes to fit her smaller feet so they could switch, except his greater weight on the flimsy snowshoes she wore would ensure his progress was even more difficult than she found it.

And…he needed to be able to move fast should something catch his eye.

Move fast to do what?

And…how was he going to do it with a splitting headache and a tendency to get dizzy if he turned too fast?

Finally spotting a downed log covered by a six-inch coverlet of snow, he stopped. He'd have liked to feel relief, but the truth was, he felt as if his shoulder had been pinned together with a rusty spike.

Ava wasn't as far behind him as he'd feared. She lifted each foot in an exaggerated move and strode forward without hesitation, her concentration intense enough she was only a few feet away when she noticed he'd stopped and did the same.

She shuffled forward, planted her improvised poles and shrugged the pack off her back. Zach grabbed it with his good arm and lowered it to the log.

"We should see our tracks from yesterday anytime," he said.

She grimaced. "That'll have to be an improvement."

"Yeah." He sat down carefully, and she did the same. "I wish it would snow."

"Not likely this late in the season, but—" She tipped her head back and gazed at the sky. Seeing the same thing he had, she said, "I didn't pay any attention this morning, but that cloud cover does have a certain look to it."

Glad she'd confirmed his instincts, he said, "A few inches would hide our tracks."

"Not just behind us, but ahead, too."

"Right. If we can keep going even if it's coming down hard…"

"They might conceivably think we were buried in the avalanche. Except…"

She'd seen the fatal flaw.

"We're taking the logical route out of the mountains. They'll be behind us, and able to move faster."

"Unless they kept going along the ridge."

He hoped she couldn't hear the deep apprehension in his voice. "And are maybe waiting ahead for us. Yeah."

Zach hated being the walnut that would be crushed by the nutcracker. The situation was familiar to him, but this time he was as vulnerable as any civilian, and needing to protect Ava besides.

"You holding up okay?" he finally asked. They'd been on their way a ridiculously short length of time and shouldn't have stopped, but, damn, he hurt, and she was having to work at least twice as hard as usual to make any progress.

"Fine. And it so happens…" She raised her eyebrows. "I carry ace bandages."

Zach found a grin for her. "Mary Poppins."

Ava's laugh lit her face. Damn, she was beautiful, bruises and all. He couldn't look away. He wasn't sure what she saw on his face, but wariness stole her amusement. She proceeded to dig in her pack, finally producing a red canvas bag with the classic Red Cross symbol on it.

He pressed his upper arm to his side. "Do your worst."

That earned him a distracted smile as she unrolled the first stretchy bandage. "I think I'll need to use both. These are designed for a knee or some such. Your chest and arm together are wide, especially when you're wearing the parka."

Zach held still as she stretched the bandage over his arm just above the elbow, then across his back and chest. There wasn't much overlap, but she fastened it securely, then duplicated her effort with the second bandage.

"I'm not sure it'll hold if you yank against it," she said doubtfully.

"I'll try to be good."

"You inspire me with confidence."

Hearing her teasing, he smiled again. "I have my moments."

Her chuckle warmed him. "Wait—I think there's some cord left that's about the right length."

She was right. He just hoped they could untie the sturdier cord when they needed to.

With his movements even more hindered, Zach was irritated to discover how little help he could give her, even with something as simple as lifting her pack and slipping her arms through the straps.

She didn't say anything when he set out again, figuring he should pick out a path given his vastly lighter and stronger snowshoes. Plucky as she was, she stayed close behind, although she had at least a couple of mishaps in the next few minutes, judging from her under-her-breath grumbling. He probably swore a couple of times himself as he adjusted to the even more limited range of motion, as well as moments of double vision.

He'd been right, fortunately; maybe ten minutes later, he saw their tracks veer up gradually to cross the formerly open bowl of land. Those tracks ended abruptly at the edge of the now impassable mass of snow, rocks and ice.

Which would slow their pursuers down considerably if they came this way.

Zach would have said that he and Ava had

been unbelievably lucky, except their survival wasn't all due to chance. Contrary to his original incredulity at the sight of a lone woman traveling in these mountains, Ava had planned well. She'd escaped the avalanche because she'd made the smart choice to prepare, and had had the presence of mind to trigger her airbag. *He'd* survived because of her determination—and because she'd brought the probe and folding shovel she'd needed to find and dig him out.

He liked everything that told him about her.

Zach gave a last, frustrated look back, wishing there'd been some way he could have held on to that damned pack, and told himself to give it up.

With the going becoming easier, he waved her ahead of him. This way he didn't have to constantly look back to judge her pace and see whether she was struggling. She was unlikely to notice his brief stops to clear the dizziness.

Initially glad they both wore parkas and pants in shades of green and gray that blended with the foliage, he began to wish they wore white, like the men on the ridge had. Zach had seen a documentary about the Tenth Mountain Division fighting in World War II. They'd been mobile in conditions not so different from this on Nordic skis and wearing white from head to boot. They would have moved through a blizzard like ghosts. He wondered if the terrorists—or only one terrorist and a pack of mercenaries to escort him—had gotten the idea from those mountain troops, but doubted it. All you had to do was study photos of this daunting country, glaciated and snow swathed, to see you'd blend in the best clothed in white.

Unfortunately, Ava hadn't had the least warning of any danger, and even Zach hadn't taken very seriously his buddy's suggestion he watch for anyone looking like they'd gone cross country over the Canadian border. What were the odds?

He was still stunned. There had to be hundreds, thousands, of easier places to slip across the border. Short of taking the same risks in the Rocky Mountains around Glacier National Park, this had to be one of the more challenging routes.

Which also made it one of the least patrolled, of course, especially at this time of year with the backcountry closed.

Even as he watched Ava struggle ahead of him and tried to block out his own pain, Zach did his best to frame a plan that might allow them to survive. The options were few, and shaky, unless Borisyuk and company used their heads and ran for it.

Unfortunately, his gut said that was unlikely.

PICK UP MY FOOT. Now the other one. Left. Right.

Ava focused her entire concentration on each step. It reminded her of swimming laps, when she counted how many she'd done. It worked like meditation, she'd always thought: *ten, ten, ten*—flip turn—*eleven, eleven, eleven.* No room for stress.

Left. Right.

At least now she had tracks to follow.

She had no idea how much time had passed when Zach spoke to her back. "Let's take a quick break to talk."

Surprised, she came close to stumbling but managed to right herself. There wasn't any place to sit down here; the vegetation was thick. Ava laboriously turned herself to see him looking grimmer than she liked. She hoped the expression was a result of the pain getting to him versus him having heard or seen something—

"I've been thinking."

Her heartbeat quickened.

"I'm betting they split up. Possibly the main group moved on, but sent two or three men to make sure no one survived the avalanche."

She could only stare at him.

"Those men might have started descending the ridge, but it would have been extremely difficult going. Impossible in the dark, even if they have headlamps. Either they somehow set up camp partway down—and it couldn't have been very comfortable—or they used their heads and didn't begin the descent until first light. Which means they'll be well behind us even though we didn't set off until this morning. They'll take some time to try to find evidence of anyone surviving."

"Which they will immediately."

He nodded. "Our tracks. I thought about trying to wipe them out, but it would have been painfully slow. And once the men reached the trail on their way to rejoin their group, they'd have seen that two people are moving ahead of them. They'll be able to move one hell of a lot faster than we can, too."

"But...why wouldn't they have all gone on?" She was begging, but couldn't help herself.

Muscles bunched in his jaw. "As I said before, I really doubt Grigor Borisyuk would be willing to leave a witness alive. On top of that, as a group, they were counting on going unseen. They may not have known there are stretches burned in recent forest fires where they'd be exposed. Why would they, unless they'd looked at Google images? As it is, suddenly they realized that not only had they been noticed, but the person watching them wasn't just seeing small figures from a great distance. She had the kind of lens that meant she *really* saw them. Put yourself in their shoes. They'd be desperate to get under cover. What if she—and that's assuming they realized you're a woman—was in radio contact with someone? If a spotting plane or helicopter passed over, they'd be dead ducks or else have to take actions—say, shoot down a helicopter—that would bring even more attention to them. I believe they scuttled for tree cover, then decided to descend from the ridge to make sure the avalanche took care of you."

Ava didn't know what to say. She'd led a more adventurous life than most people, but none of that had involved human beings out to kill her. Or people who were capable of shooting down a helicopter. Thank God Zach had been close enough behind her yesterday! Otherwise, she'd be alone, unaware that the men up on the ridge had triggered the avalanche, never mind that one of them was a terrorist hunted throughout the free world. She might have figured out an even more primitive snowshoe design and set out to head back down the valley, but when those strange men caught up with her, she'd have no idea that they intended to kill her.

A shudder rattled her, one Zach saw. His eyes narrowed. "Ava?"

"You don't think they saw you."

"I doubt it." He hesitated. "Once they spot our tracks, though…"

They'd know there were two of them.

She nodded numbly. "It still looks like it might snow." But it hadn't. She let that go. "You're saying we need to really hurry."

He was watching her intently as he hesitated. "Yes, for now. If we keep moving, I doubt they can catch up with us today. The closer we can get to being able to call for help, the better."

She was torturously slow. It was like the turtle and the hare. No, a bicyclist on the freeway being chased by a sports car that didn't even have to exceed the speed limit to go sixty miles in an hour to the cyclist's…what? Five miles? Ten?

Zach had to know how far they really were from being able to call anyone at all. But that had to be their goal. If they could reach a point where the vee of the valley widened and a few alternate trails separated from the main one, she wouldn't feel quite so trapped.

"Then…then you think we can hide?" she asked.

"I hope I can find someplace off the trail to set up camp for the night."

And then what?

His expression hardened. "After that, at some point my goal will be to hide *you*. If I can take down even one of those men, I'll be armed. I may be able to arm you. That changes the odds."

Horrified, she opened her mouth, then closed it. Those odds sounded *abysmal* to her. She decided not to bother pointing out that she'd never in her life fired a gun, and she wouldn't remind him that he was already injured. So he'd been a soldier; how much combat experience did Zach actually have?

"I hate that idea," she said, straight out, "but I don't have any alternative to suggest."

A nerve twitched in his cheek and his eyes softened. "I'm not wild about it, either, but I think our only chance is to go on the offensive."

She lifted her chin. "Right now, we'd better get moving."

"Afraid so."

Ava shuffled back around so that she was pointing south, more or less, and picked up her right foot. Then left.

Trying to run would be a mistake, she felt

sure, but she was in good physical condition. She'd increase her pace.

Right foot. Left. Right.

HE'D SEEN HOW she blanched at his plan, but clearly, crumbling in fear wasn't in Ava Brevick's nature. He should have asked whether she'd done any target shooting, but he could do that later. It was safe to say that a wildlife photographer didn't hunt wildlife as a hobby, which meant any experience she had handling guns was extremely limited.

That didn't mean she wouldn't pull a trigger if she had to.

Don't get ahead of yourself, he reminded himself. *Keep a sharp eye out, both ahead and behind. Think about how an unarmed man could set up an ambush.* Once he had her in hiding, he'd have her remove the ace bandages and cords strapping his arm to his body. It would be bad if the arm left the shoulder socket again because he hadn't given it time to heal, but sometimes you just had to gamble.

He couldn't help second-guessing himself. If they could have stayed completely hidden at the foot of the avalanche, maybe the group would have been satisfied and gone on their way. Sure, he and Ava would have been short on food, but humans could go on for a long time with nothing to eat.

Only—what if they'd made a single mistake? Say, missed a track one or the other of them had made below the foot of the avalanche? Dropped something from Ava's pack?

We'd be dead.

If the terrorists hadn't headed south on the ridge as fast as they could go, which was the smart thing to do, he reminded himself.

Ava fell in front of him. Zach helped her up and crouched to examine her snowshoe, pulling off his gloves to tighten the strap designed to hold her boot in place. Straightening, he said, "I wish…" but made himself break off.

His father would have growled, *Wishes are horses, boy, and you don't know how to ride. Life's hard. You need to be hard, too.*

He shook his head slightly. *Thanks, Dad.* No, his father had never, in Zach's memory, been anything Zach would call loving, kind, supportive. He hadn't ditched the kids he didn't seem to have any use for, though, and maybe the toughness he'd taught had been useful, in the end. Someday Zach would have to ask his brother and sister what they thought about it.

"You wish?" Ava prompted softly.

"Nothing helpful, I'm afraid."

She offered him a twisted smile. "I wish, too." Then she set out again, giving no indication she'd twisted a knee or ankle during any of these falls, or was suffering from the massive bruising she must have acquired courtesy of being flung down a long, steep slope by a behemoth of snow and ice.

Chapter Six

Every hour or two, he insisted they stop. She moved steadily, but he watched for tiny falters and would call a break. He chafed at their speed, but wasn't sure he'd have done that much better on his own without full use of his upper body. Twice he took more ibuprofen, too, for what good it did—especially since it exacerbated his nausea—and insisted she swallow some, too. He was grateful for all her preparations, especially the fact that she'd tossed a full bottle of pain reliever into her pack.

At what he deemed to be lunchtime, he spotted a decent place for them to sit down.

"We'd better have a bite to eat," he said.

"I'm…not really hungry."

If she was lying because she worried about them running out of food, that was one thing. If she really *wasn't* hungry, that was cause to worry given their extreme energy expenditure.

What if she, too, had suffered a head injury she hadn't mentioned?

He was the one to dig in her pack for the individual packets of nuts and dried fruits. He opened one of each for her and poured them into her gloved hand. She stared down incomprehensibly for a minute, then to his relief started to eat.

He followed suit, chasing down a couple of bites with a drink of water before handing her the bottle.

For a moment, he only listened to the silence. The sky felt heavier, almost oppressive, but not a single flake of snow had yet fallen.

"You travel a good part of the year?" he asked, going for conversational in part to hide his intense curiosity.

"Oh…more like three or four months out of the year. Choosing and editing the photos I want to use is time-consuming, and I have to market myself, too."

"Where do you live?"

"Right now, Colorado." Her shoulders moved. "I spend some time with…a friend in Maine." Her pause was almost infinitesimal. "Whales have become something of a specialty of mine. Oh, and my roommate from college is in Florida."

Was the friend in Maine a man? Ridiculous to dislike the idea so intensely.

All he let himself say was, "So when you need a little sunshine…?"

Her expression had become livelier. "Exactly. Plus…lots of wildlife in Florida."

He groaned and stretched. "I hate to say it—"

"No, you're right." She hastily zipped up her pack, eased herself into it and stood. "We shouldn't have stopped."

"I'm the one who insisted," he said mildly.

"I know, but… You'd be faster without me. Don't deny it. I'm fine, though. I can keep going as long as we need to."

"Yeah." He was already talking to her back as she took a first step, lifting her foot in that crude snowshoe high. He even believed her.

HER ENTIRE BODY HURT. Every bruise, every wrenched joint, every insulted muscle made themselves felt. Ava tried to remember the fluid stride that carried her along before. She capitalized the word: *Before*. It was as if she was a different woman now, in the After. Desperately fleeing for her life.

Right foot. Left. Right.

Trusting a man. A stranger.

No choice.

Her chest burned, her every breath seared until it froze as she released it. Her shoulders… She didn't even want to think about her shoulders. Half the time, the pole sank too deep, making her lurch; she stabbed each one forward, preparing for the next stride, with growing trepidation.

Her thighs and even her butt burned, too. Her feet and ankles hurt, which was new; having to lift the makeshift snowshoes higher than usual wasn't part of her practiced stride, the one that worked for snowshoeing as well as it did for running.

Right foot. Left. Right. Left.

She clung to the mantra, using it to— mostly—drown out the pain. The fear, too. Because this was all she *could* do: keep going, as fast as possible without breaking one of the snowshoes and slowing them down for as long as it would take Zach to make a new one.

She kept her teeth clenched, too, to hold back the faintest of whimpers. He was certainly stronger than her, but the shoulder injury trumped all her relatively minor aches and pains. And he had those, too, Ava didn't doubt. Maybe more than that. A couple of times, she'd thought his eyes looked as dazed as they had when she first dug him out of the snow. He did some odd blinking, too. Whatever was bothering him, she hadn't heard a single groan or bout of muffled swearing coming from back there.

"It's snowing."

Right. Left. Right.

She picked up her left foot, then had to think before she set it down. Her rhythm was broken. What had he just said?

She blinked a few times. A big, fat snowflake drifted down toward her nose. Going cross-eyed, she watched it continue on its way until it settled on her parka, remaining visible for a long moment.

Ava raised her face to the sky and saw not just a few stray flakes of snow descending, but enough to muffle the impact of the green of the trees surrounding them.

She twisted in place, so she didn't have to bother laboriously shifting her snowshoes. "It's snowing!"

His grin blazed at her. "Didn't believe me, huh?"

"Oh, my God! I *can't* believe it."

He shuffled forward until he was almost stepping on the back of her snowshoes, reached a big, gloved hand around her nape and planted an exuberant quick, kiss on her mouth. "Someone is on our side."

Shaking off the effect of his cold lips, warm

breath and the smile that made her heart jump, Ava said, "I hope it keeps on and buries our tracks."

"But doesn't drop two or three feet and bury *us*."

She wrinkled her nose.

Zach nodded ahead. "I hate to say it—"

She hated it every time he said that, but nodded. They had to keep moving, take advantage of being able to follow their own track as long as possible, because if the snow continued to fall, eventually they'd lose it. After that, finding the trail at all would be as hard as it had been when she traversed it days ago. Harder, if the snow kept falling, reducing visibility.

As she took the first step and then the second—*right, left, right again*—she wished vengefully that the men who might or might not be pursuing them weren't used to traveling on foot in a snowy, mountainous landscape.

Although... Russia had plenty of that, didn't it? Why couldn't this group have come from a sunbaked part of the world where the biggest challenge from nature was sandstorms?

THEY KEPT MOVING as long as Zach thought they dared. Longer. Not only couldn't he see any hint of a track ahead now, the quality of light was changing. He found it harder to make out the falling snow against the deepening sky.

The entire way, he searched their surroundings for a possible open spot well off the trail that wouldn't be painfully obvious to a passerby. A couple of times, he made some effort to give the impression they might have turned off, if only to briefly slow down any pursuers. He had no trouble catching up with Ava, and he wasn't even sure she'd noticed what he was doing.

They had crossed a stretch that was more open than he liked—a long-ago remnant of another avalanche or wildfire—then plunged back into the more typical, tangled vegetation he was really growing to detest. At the moment, he couldn't see or hear the river, although it lay off to their right.

He still hadn't picked up anything from behind them, but Ava was noticeably flagging when he finally saw what he'd been looking for.

"Hold up," he said.

She stopped so fast, he almost stepped on the tails of her snowshoes.

"Let me check this out." He stepped cautiously toward the river, able to slide between a thick growth of willows and alders and heaven knows what else. He bet this was, or had been, a game trail. Not obvious, but passable. If he could find a flat place large enough for them to set up the tent…

Ten minutes within what felt like a frozen jungle, he saw what he sought. He poked with his crude poles. No, this wasn't flat ground perfect for a campsite; there seemed to be a snarl of dormant growth below the snow, but he wasn't feeling real picky about where he laid his—their—sleeping bag right now, and he bet Ava would agree. Some nice, low branches of the cedar he'd just circled would veil them from anyone more than a few feet away, just as they'd been in last night's campsite.

He tipped his head, picking up the murmur of running water. A distant *crack* was easily identifiable, too: a branch breaking beneath a heavy load of wet snow. They'd hear that sound all night. Speaking of—

He took out the knife he'd pilfered from her pack and cut off a couple of stiff cedar branches.

Carrying them, remaining careful with each step, he made his way back to Ava.

"I found a place to set up camp for the night. I'd like to not break any of the vegetation—" he gripped some shrubby alder in his gloved hands "—if we can help it. I could carry you—"

She set her jaw. "Don't be silly."

"Okay. Follow my track."

She did, every movement exaggerated, gingerly. Satisfied, he turned to go backward, following her and using his branches to obliterate the tracks they were laying. Bending over, a couple of times he felt close to passing out. Had to be done. At the rate the snow still fell, he felt sure that within half an hour, their passage would no longer be visible.

By the time he caught up with her, satisfied, she'd slipped her feet from the snowshoes, set them against a nearby branch, removed her pack and taken out a tarp to lay across the snow. Tent next. She didn't argue when he helped her erect the thing, although it was easier than any tent he'd ever slept in. She half crawled in and unrolled the thin foam pad. Despite everything, he admired her taut butt in tight-fitting pants as it waggled before she turned for the sleeping bag. He set his snowshoes right next to hers and, one-handed, hauled the pack inside the tent.

Darkness had been falling with astonishing speed. Already he had trouble making out her features with any clarity. Last night, he'd had too much on his mind to be as aware of how cramped the quarters were. He couldn't shrink himself, but he suspected she wouldn't have cared if they'd had half the space.

He sat his butt down on the foot of the sleeping bag, letting her take the top. "Now if we just had a Jacuzzi."

"Room service."

He grimaced. "I'd settle for a hot shower." Yeah, he felt sure he didn't smell sweet right now. He'd worry more, except she'd been at least as long away from a last shower or bath as he was.

For what had to be a couple of minutes, neither of them moved or spoke. He felt as if they were inside a room designed and built to be soundproof. His eardrums felt odd.

"I'm starved," Ava said. "Do you think we can use the stove?"

"Yeah. We can set it up right at the opening here. We could both use an actual meal. We need—" He broke off. He didn't have to tell her that they needed to be strong tomorrow. For the moment, they could revel in the release in tension.

Assuming that was possible when stopping made him aware of every aching muscle, as well as the deep throbbing in his abused shoulder. At least his head was grateful for his stillness.

"Can you help me unwrap my arm?" he asked.

"Oh! Sure. It actually held all day."

He smiled crookedly at her. "It did. Solid construction."

Her laugh made him feel triumphant.

She scooted close to him, peeled off her gloves and picked apart the cord and then unfastened the two ace bandages. Then she very carefully rolled them up again before setting them aside.

He might let her put them back on in the morning—he thought he'd had some relief from the limited range of motion—but he couldn't hamper himself when he went on the offensive, so maybe it wasn't worth wearing them for what, if they were lucky, might be only a few hours.

Zach had no doubt that tomorrow was the day.

Unless, of course, he reminded himself for the umpteenth time, the whole party had stayed along the ridge and either continued on their merry way, or set up in wait for the survivor(s) of the avalanche. In that case, he guessed he and Ava would meet up with Borisyuk and company the day after tomorrow.

He needed to prepare for either possibility, but his gut said somebody was tracking them already.

ZACH RELUCTANTLY GAVE her permission to do the cooking. Ava hid rolled eyes from him.

Sensing how intensely protective he felt for her, she wouldn't wish herself in this situation with a different kind of man. Or alone, God forbid. On the other hand, she wondered how controlling Zach would be on a day-to-day basis in normal life. Did he ever let up?

Well, she'd never find out. This intense closeness was temporary. It wasn't as if they had any kind of relationship that would go anywhere. They'd part ways; him back to western Washington, her to Colorado. Home, only it didn't quite feel that way.

All of this was assuming they both survived the next several days, of course.

She didn't even ask him for his meal preference, given how limited options were. She freeze-dried the meals for trips herself, and was rather proud of how good she'd gotten at it. Tonight, they were having teriyaki chicken with brown rice.

Zach thanked her when she handed him her one dish and a fork, leaving her to eat out of the pan using a spoon. He took a bite and looked up.

"Damn, this is good. Doesn't taste much like the MREs I'm used to."

"I'm assuming that's the military version of my meals?"

"Yeah." He took a couple more bites, obviously savoring each one. "In theory, they're better than they used to be. In practice... I'd usually prefer just about anything else."

"What kind of soldier were you?" she asked. "Or...no, I suppose you'd have said sailor if you'd been navy."

"Or airman if I'd served in the air force," he agreed. "I was an army ranger in the regiment that does special operations."

Her lips formed the words "spec ops."

"Yeah, constant action. We were...inserted in some pretty dangerous places. Rescued hostages, accomplished raids, gathered intel. I... lost a few too many friends, came back from a final injury—" he rotated his right arm—the good one—in remembrance "—and decided it was time to get out."

She just watched him.

"Which is easier said than done. They warn you, but you shrug it off."

Why was he being so open with her? Because he suspected they wouldn't live, and wanted to connect with her, the last person he could spend time with?

If that was so...she understood. Even felt the same impulse. Why hide anything from this man? Maybe...it would be freeing, to talk about some of the bad stuff. Part of her wished she could see his face, but that would mean he could see hers, and maybe talking was easier in the dark.

"Why the military?" she asked.

"My mother died when I was eight years old. Dad was career military. A colonel." Wryness sounded in his voice. "When I was being rebellious, I talked about college. He sneered at eggheads. Useless. The first to go down if violence erupted."

"Except that they invented most products he used, including weaponry," she pointed out.

"Try telling my father that."

"He's alive?"

"Yeah. We don't see much of each other. I do stay in touch with my brother and sister."

He fell quiet, leaving her to fill in the blanks, of which there were many.

After a minute, she said, "I think I'll just use snow to wipe these dishes out. We should try to refill the bottle in the morning." When he asked, she agreed that she had some purifier tablets.

Naturally, she rejected his offer to clean up, and he conceded, letting her crawl past him and do the task. Out of the corner of his eye, she saw him lift his newly injured arm and rotate it. He caught her eye, and said, "I have a better range of motion than I would have expected. Binding my arm today was the right thing to do. With a little luck, by morning the soreness will be reduced."

She and Zach took turns to find some privacy outside before each, in turn, scrambled back into the tent. The snow still fell, although she thought more slowly now. The temperature had definitely dropped with nightfall, though. What was spring down below sure as hell wasn't here.

When he started peeling off clothes, she pretended she didn't notice. They'd slept together last night. Why she felt nervous tonight, she had no idea.

Because he'd kissed her?

Maybe, although she didn't think he'd intended it in a sexual way. She *had* seen him watching her in a way that definitely was sexual and made her tingle, though, so she shouldn't discount the kiss.

They had absolutely no choice but to sleep together. Listening to the rustles as he slid into the bag, she undressed, too. He rolled over to let her lay her clothes atop his, then rolled back over, holding the bag invitingly open.

She slithered in, squirming until she was *almost* comfortable. He was able to zip up the sleeping bag tonight, after which he adjusted her position to suit him. She'd have complained, except she was definitely comfier.

Warmer, too. His big body radiated heat in a way hers didn't.

"Okay?" he murmured.

"Mmm-hmm."

As tired as she was, she couldn't imagine falling asleep immediately. She'd never been so aware of a man's body stretched out against hers, even on the few occasions she'd let anyone get that close. Of course, she wanted to move, to rub against him, to—

She told herself to knock it off. This was nothing but a reaction to the possibility that they might both die tomorrow. *Have some pride.*

Anyway, *he* wasn't doing a thing but lying there, his breathing completely even. He was no closer to sleep than she was.

"Tell me about you," he said after a moment. "Is this friend in Maine a guy?"

Talking. What could be a better distraction?

"No. Eileen is—" Oh, why not just tell him? "We went through two foster homes together. Aged out of the system and graduated from high school together, too. We've…stayed close."

"How long were you in the foster care system?" The low rumble of his voice, felt as well as heard, was more comforting than she would ever have expected.

"From the time I was a feral seven-year-old on. Nobody considered me adoptable, and I was difficult enough, so I got moved over and over."

She couldn't miss the sudden tension in the muscles supporting and enclosing her. "Feral?"

Ava had never, as an adult, told anyone this.

"My mother had drug problems. She just didn't come back one day. I...waited for a long time, then finally went looking for her. I was on my own for a while. Maybe as much as a year. No one, including me, knows. Turns out everyone assumed she and I had taken off, so nobody was looking for me. The house was vacant, after all. I was...too scared to look for help, I think. The stuff we left behind, well, no one would want it, anyway. Mom had never enrolled me in school. I didn't know any adults who weren't addicts. A cop pounced on me one day. I kept the picture they took of me when he hauled me in. I was skin and bones and filthy, and had this wild bush of hair. I hardly looked human."

After a long, fraught silence, Zach said in a constrained voice, "I've seen kids like that. In other parts of the world."

She bobbed her head, knowing he'd feel that. "Well, I got cleaned up, tutored so I caught up in school. Humanized. You know. Still, Eileen was the first person I really bonded with, and we were both fourteen by then. She'd been abused. I guess…we understood each other. That foster home wasn't so great, but a social worker rescued us, and we spent our last three years with a really great older couple. It gave me an idea what home might feel like."

"You still in touch with them?"

"Yes." John and Alice still treated the two of them like daughters, just way younger than their biological ones. They meant a lot to Ava, had maybe been her salvation.

"And the photography?"

"That was actually from an earlier foster home. The wife was a news photographer for a local paper. She saw how interested I was and gave me my first camera. I was hooked. At the time, it was way better than phone cameras. I never looked back."

It was true. She still thought about Jennifer long after most of her foster parents' faces and names had blurred. Someday, she should get in touch with her to say thanks, even if Jennifer and her husband had dumped Ava, too, at the first hint of problems.

"I want to hurt somebody for you," Zach said, in a voice that wasn't quite as expressionless as he probably intended, "but it's way too late, isn't it?"

"Yes. I'm…okay."

"Are you?" he asked softly, but not as if he expected an answer.

She didn't give him one.

Chapter Seven

Zach tipped his head back to look up at the sky. A few snowflakes still drifted down. Any and all tracks had been obscured the evening before, which was both good news and bad. His and Ava's pace was even slower this morning. He'd taken the lead instead of letting her risk her flimsy, primitive snowshoes.

Yes, anyone behind them would be moving slowly, too, but they were better equipped. He bet every single man they'd seen on that ridgetop was in excellent physical condition, prepared for winter travel in the backcountry. Unless somebody had taken a fall, none were injured, either.

He'd hoped the effects of what had to have been a concussion would have relented by this morning, but no such luck. There wasn't a damn thing he could do about it besides take the ibuprofen. That, and try to block out knowledge of his headache, a dull backdrop to the sharper shoulder pain. He consoled himself with the fact that the nausea hadn't recurred since yesterday afternoon.

He and Ava forged on for one hour, two, three. He kept an eye on his watch, glad he'd worn one. Sometime during the second hour he'd begun to feel an unpleasant but all-too-familiar itch crawling up his spine to his neck. He wanted to blame his imagination, but couldn't. He'd relied on this same feeling countless times over his years in dangerous parts of the world. It had saved his butt, and the lives of others in his unit, because he didn't let himself brush it off.

He felt like crap, but it was still time to set his plan into motion, he decided. Like yesterday, he kept a sharp eye out for anyplace he could stash Ava.

Fifteen minutes later, he thought he'd found it.

He said quietly, "Hold up," and made sure she'd stopped and sagged forward with her weight on the poles to rest. She must've guessed what he was going to do.

As he had last night, he left the trail, doing his best to stay on top of all the low-growing, tangled growth beneath the snow that wanted to snag his snowshoes, while pushing through the ubiquitous willows and alder and branches of smaller evergreens. Once again, he moved with extra care so as not to break a branch that would catch the eye of anyone looking for signs of human passage. An enormous log, the tree a real old-timer, had fallen about twenty feet from the trail. Given that it hadn't yet rotted enough to start service as a nurse log for countless seedling trees, he'd been lucky to notice it. What he was hoping...

Where the roots would once have been torn from the earth, he started probing with one of his poles. It immediately plunged deep. *Yes.* He couldn't feel any shrubbery filling in the hole yet, either. Probably it had come down as recently as this winter.

He turned and realized he could barely see Ava where she waited. The trick would be wiping out any trace of her passage—and his both going and coming. He hoped she wasn't given to flashbacks, since he'd have to leave her sunken in a well filled with snow, but he had faith in her resilience.

"This will do," he said aloud.

"Should I...?"

He'd carry her, he decided. He suspected her snowshoes wouldn't hold up to easing through such thick growth. They couldn't afford for her to fall and break branches off.

"Wait for me," he called, and began gingerly edging his way back to her.

It probably wasn't even noon yet, he realized. Maybe they could go on farther…but if he were Borisyuk, he wouldn't tolerate less than his own zeal in his underlings. Once again, Zach had deemed it futile to try to erase the tracks he and Ava had made.

The tracks between the trail where she waited and where he planned to stow her—those, he thought he could make less noticeable. Once he set out on his own, all he had to do was shuffle a little here and there to make it appear as if there were still two of them.

Or, he'd turn around and go back. He'd seen a couple of places that he thought would lend themselves to the ambush he had in mind.

Any way you looked at it, this was a long shot. His only real chance was if they'd sent a scout on ahead, knowing how much noise a group their size would make.

One man he could take out. Seven or eight at the same time, no.

The fact that there was only one path they could have taken made him and Ava incredibly vulnerable. On the other hand, short of continuing on the ridge, the bad guys had the same limitation.

He was gambling that he had guessed right,

and Borisyuk had sent only two or three men down to check out the avalanche while the rest of them proceeded on the planned route. It made sense. Delivering Borisyuk safely into the US was the primary goal, chasing what might turn out to be shadows secondary.

He still suspected that the main group would be waiting at the foot of the river valley. But Zach had enough confidence to believe that, if he could whittle the numbers down and, by so doing, arm and provision the two of them, he and Ava would have a good chance. How much actual combat experience would a group of mercenaries have? If they had any, it might have been gained invading Ukraine, and that wasn't the kind of warfare that would serve them here.

Right now…he had to go with his gut, and he had to give Ava the best chance to live if he couldn't return to her.

So FOCUSED ON plodding forward—*left, right, left*—Ava had almost forgotten Zach's intentions until he'd ordered her to stop. When he emerged from the entangled growth to tell her he would be leaving her here, terror choked her.

"But—"

The expression in his dark eyes was both

kind and implacable. "We talked about this. There are not a lot of choices here."

"But…they could kill you."

"People have tried before. Now, come on."

He insisted on carrying first the pack then her through that vicious, scratchy growth. No man had ever slung her up in his arms like this. She wanted to struggle, knowing he couldn't feel much better than she did, but only held on tight to limit how much of her weight he had to support with his left arm. She kept her eyes fixed on his throat and stubbled jaw, which were generally not revealing. Once he set her back on her feet, she couldn't see what he had in mind.

"There's a big hole here." He stabbed his pole in a few times to demonstrate. "See that root bole there? It was torn out of the ground. This hole could be six or eight feet deep, maybe more. We're going to dig out enough for you to make a nest, then I'll build a wall of snow and try to make it look natural. If they're not familiar with old-growth forests, they won't know what they're looking at."

"And… I just *wait*? I don't understand how you think you can overcome even one heavily armed man, never mind several!" Did that sound hysterical? She didn't care. "You're hurt. I can tell."

"I know what I'm doing. Trust me."

Ava didn't argue for long. She grasped the shovel and began to dig out a mountain of soft snow, trying to envision the hole as an igloo.

"Let me look through your pack," he said absently, as if he might find—what?—a 9mm handgun she'd forgotten to mention? All she saw him pocket were the remaining pieces of line, a couple of stretchy bungee cords, the telescoped probe and, once he was satisfied at the depth of the hole, the shovel. Then, rising to his feet, he looked at her.

"Spread the tarp as a bottom layer. Wrap yourself in the sleeping bag. Use extra clothes if you have to. Staying warm will be your biggest challenge." His gaze was intense. "Nibble on food. Be quiet, whether you hear anything that worries you or not. Got it?"

"Yes, but—"

"I'll come back for you."

She had to ask, her voice on the verge of cracking. "What if you can't? How long do I wait?"

His mouth tightened. "At least today. Better through tomorrow. By that time, my guess is they'll have given up looking for you."

"Then why don't both of us—"

He shook his head. "They know by now that *someone* is ahead of them. If they get their hands on me, they may decide they weren't following two people after all. How could they ever find you?"

"But—"

"We need weapons if we're going to make it."

Hearing no give at all, Ava gritted her teeth to keep them from chattering. This was the worst thing he could have asked her to do, but he was right. She'd be a hindrance rather than a help when it came to trying to take down an armed combatant. He'd be so worried about her, he wouldn't be able to concentrate on what he needed to do.

"Yes. Okay."

He took her hand, presumably intending to help lower her into the pit, but went very still.

"Ava."

The intensity in his eyes was still there, but now he was utterly focused on her face. His gaze flicked to her lips. He bent slowly.

She suddenly wanted nothing so much in the world as for him to kiss her. Grabbing his parka with both hands, she pushed up on tip-toe. She met his mouth clumsily, but didn't care. Despite the cold, and the fact that he wore heavy gloves, he cupped her jaw and tipped her head to an angle that let him warm her lips, taste them, part them. She welcomed his tongue, tried to block out everything but this moment.

Which worked until he groaned, took his mouth from hers and leaned his forehead on hers instead.

"Ava." His chest rose and fell fast, hard. "We have to do this."

Her eyes burned, and she averted her face. "I know." As an excuse to avoid looking at him, she slid down into the hole, pulled the tarp from her pack and spread it, then sat down.

He already had the shovel in his hand, and in mere moments had shaped the pile of snow from the hole into a long, smooth rampart that even from her perspective could have been new-fallen snow atop a log.

He looked down at her, and it was all she could do not to let him see her fear.

"Be careful," she whispered.

He nodded, said, "I'll be back," and disappeared.

She heard him for a few minutes, brushing the snow so that no one could detect the path back out to the main trail.

And then she was alone in a hole that could have been dug out for a coffin.

Zach decided to go back the way they'd come. When the first guy he intended to take on saw the returning track, he'd guess the person, or two people, he was pursuing had hit an impassable obstacle and were seeking another route. Since the actual trail was buried under snow, it would be easy to wander off it.

Except that those opportunities were few and far between, given the rampant growth in a river valley deep in a temperate rainforest. But one thing Zach felt sure of: these guys weren't from around here.

He hesitated briefly at the first spot he'd seen to believably turn off. Part of him wanted to go on, to set up this confrontation as far as possible from Ava, but he couldn't risk suddenly coming face-to-face with one of these guys. Plus, he needed to hoard his strength as much as he could.

The way was initially easy enough; he guessed it was a kind of spur off the main trail. Could be an animal trail, or ground worn by the feet of hikers deciding to take a break and have a bite to eat at a particularly pretty place beside the small, tumbling river.

He walked as far as the river bank, then circled around to set up by a particularly bushy group of small trees to serve as a blind. His chosen location was out of sight of the main trail—its other primary benefit.

Once he set out on the hunt, he became the soldier he'd once been, emotions buried, his mind occupied with imagining every possible outcome to every choice he made. In the end, he was left with his original plan.

He constructed his snare out of a couple of whips of willows, pulled across the way and knotted to the base of other wiry growth. Just in case his prey didn't fall for the first trap— he'd have to lift his snowshoes extra high at that particular spot—Zach crouched a couple of feet farther on to lay a second snare with one of the bungee cords he'd taken from Ava's pack. Then he stood to shake a couple of strategically placed evergreen boughs so that snow tumbled over the snares. Just enough to hide them. Natural seeming. If he or Ava had come this way, they could easily have brushed those branches. A deer could have done the same.

Then he chose where to wait, ready to spring. When the moment came, he couldn't hesitate. A single shot taken would alert all of those *other* heavily armed men, up and down the valley.

Zach was going to do his hunting as silently as was humanly possible.

IF YOU LEARNED one thing in special ops, it was patience. Hide or disguise yourself, and wait. The bursts of violence or hurry-up-and-go were scattered between long periods of waiting. He hadn't felt the humming tension in a long time, but it was familiar.

Eyes and ears sharp, he allowed his mind to drift, mainly to Ava but also to Borisyuk's agenda. Was he here for a single assassination, a death that would throw government and politics into disarray, or a high-ranking military officer whose insights and influence had become inconvenient for whomever had hired an assassin? Or had he been brought here for his bomb-making skills, the intended targets more plentiful?

Zach did wonder, and not for the first time, whether he could have imagined seeing the sought-after terrorist in that photo. If he hadn't just been shown the one-and-only previous photo of the guy and been asked to watch for him, would he have taken such a wild leap?

Since he had plenty of time, he ran through the same logic, the same arguments, that had convinced him in the first place. An especially distinctive face. The weaponry those men carried. That they'd fired an RPG to take out an innocent backcountry snowshoer who was no threat to them.

Because Ava's camera with the huge lens *was* a threat more significant than an automatic rifle.

Even if Zach had leaped to a conclusion about the one ugly face with singular features, why *did* those men sneak across the Canadian border into the US? What did they plan to do with more armaments than a typical army ranger unit carried? Why had they determined to set off an avalanche to take out one person who should have been too far away to disturb them? An innocent, at that?

It didn't add up to anything good.

If nobody showed up in pursuit, he might reshuffle his logic. He'd still believe somebody would be waiting for them where they emerged from the valley. And if that wasn't true—well, he'd call his buddy to show him Ava's photo.

His thoughts slipped, as they did every few minutes, to Ava. He had hated walking away from her. If he got back to find her dead because someone had stumbled on her... He wasn't sure he could live with that. This woman had gotten to him with stunning speed. She'd become a trusted teammate. But Ava was more because she was also a beautiful woman who had unhesitatingly shared the warmth of her body with him to save his life. She blushed when he betrayed his desire for her, which suggested she was having those same thoughts.

And last night, she'd decoded the mysteries of her personality for him, clawing him up inside. If she never showed him the photograph of the feral, hopeless child she'd been, it didn't matter. He could see it, blue eyes wild in the face of any of those skin-and-bone children clinging to life in war-torn parts of the globe.

He hadn't had to ask why she photographed nature and animals instead of humans. Or why photography, he thought now, defined her life.

He still didn't hear voices, however soft, or the shush-shush of snowshoes. He and Ava could have gone on for another hour or two—but if they had, he might not have found as perfect a place to hide her.

If I'm wrong... But the twang between his shoulder blades hadn't relented.

AVA HAD NEVER listened harder in her life. But then, what else could she do? Stare up at the sky, where she once saw the impossibly distant contrail of a jet, another time a bald eagle sweeping against the pale gray backdrop? Imagine the now scattered snowflakes coming more frequently? Envisioning herself, literally buried in snow, completed the horror she felt as she waited.

Would a gunshot be the first unnatural sound she heard? Careless voices as some of those men tramped past on the trail, oblivious to her presence? Or would it be her name, in Zach's velvet-deep voice?

Please let that be it.

Obedient because he was right, she made

herself nibble occasionally on peanuts and dried fruit. Sip the water that tasted of the tablet that had purified it. Keep her joints limber with small movements. Shiver and readjust so she could unroll the pad to lift her butt farther off the snow. Huddle, wrapped in the sleeping bag, and not let herself even *think* about climbing out of the hole and going looking for him.

After all, she knew how well *that* worked. She'd never uncovered so much as a trace of what had happened to her mother, not as a child, not as an adult.

But…*could* she make herself stay right here, alone, the rest of the day, and then the night, and then another day?

Ava didn't know.

Crack.

She tensed, even as she knew that wasn't a gunshot, only another tree limb giving way beneath the weight of snow. Head back, she glanced warily around, but didn't see any that would drop on her.

She heard a woodpecker at work, saw what she thought was a peregrine falcon soar overhead. A gray jay and a raven took turns sitting on a branch to study her, heads tipping first one way and then the other. Thank goodness a vulture didn't arrive to contemplate how much lifespan she had left. *Were* there any vultures in the North Cascades? She was pretty sure not, which made sense; in these perpetually damp woods, bodies decomposed quickly without help.

At that point, she descended into the kind of morose thoughts she abhorred. Still, it was probably inevitable to ask herself, who would even notice if she disappeared, never to be seen again?

Eventually Eileen, of course, but Eileen knew Ava was on assignment, off in some remote location without cell phone coverage. Post-trip she often plunged into editing her film, too, and forgot to even check voice mail. It would be a couple of months before Eileen would really worry.

Laura would wonder, of course; almost every winter Ava spent a couple of weeks with her in Florida, but they went long stretches without communicating the rest of the year. Plus, since Ava's last visit in January, Laura's boyfriend had moved in with her, which had made Ava wonder if staying with her for more than a night or two at a time wouldn't be awkward now.

John and Alice, but she'd spent Christmas with them so recently, and they, too, were used to long silences.

Some of the editors Ava worked with— except for Richard Vickers, who'd set up the funding for this trip and would be puzzled and irritated and possibly even litigious if she didn't submit the promised photos—would give her passing thought and start buying work from other photographers.

What a sad list that was. And really, did she care if a bunch of people out there wailed and beat their breasts at the word that she was presumed dead?

She gazed up at the sky, blinked away a snowflake and thought, *No*. She just wished there was one person who was more to her than an occasional phone call or visit, who would know *immediately* if something was wrong. Who truly loved her.

That wish feeling like a fist in her chest, she knew she had to try harder to open herself to relationships once she got out of here. No, there weren't a lot of men like Zach Reeves around, but maybe she could find one of them.

And then she growled, not quite silently. Oh, for gracious sake! She didn't do self-pity and wasn't going to start now. Of course she'd make it home! If she had to, she could wait as long as she needed to.

A greater truth crept into her consciousness: She had faith Zach *would* come back for her. Maybe that was foolish, when she'd known him such a short time, but this certainty felt bone deep.

Right now, the best thing she could do was hold on to it.

Chapter Eight

Zach moved often enough to keep from stiffening up. He rolled his shoulders, evaluating his pain level and dismissing it. He snacked a couple of times on dried fruit rather than the nuts he'd left with Ava; the fruit wouldn't crunch under his teeth. He hoped she was following his instructions.

One side of his mouth crooked up. "Advice" was a better word. In general, he doubted Ava was a woman who'd appreciate being given orders.

Despite himself, restlessness grew. Maybe he wasn't as patient as he used to be. Probably lucky he'd retired—

Swish, swish, swish.

He stiffened. The sound was subtle, not close. Rhythmic, though—and exactly what he'd been listening for.

Swish, swish, swish.

He turned his head, peering through branches

toward the main trail. There were no voices, not so much as a grunt. That sounded like a single snowshoer, although he might be mistaken. Would the man see the turnoff at all, or be too focused on what was directly ahead? If he did, Zach was still undecided about his course.

No, the guy couldn't be that foolish.

Swish, swish, swish. Getting closer.

Slower, too. Hesitating.

Zach rolled his shoulders, flexed his fingers a few more times and crouched.

Silence.

Then a few tentative sounds. The obvious track of one or maybe two snowshoers that Zach had laid was proving irresistible.

The swishing sound resumed, but quieter, as if the man was stepping carefully. He couldn't tiptoe, but he was doing his best. Ah, there he was, appearing around the bend. Clad in white, head to toe—yes, including the hood and cape that covered his backpack—but for the black automatic rifle slung to one side that clashed. Zach eyed the poles greedily. Those would be a big improvement.

No hint that the guy had company. If he did, they must be spread out.

Zach had already divested himself of his snowshoes. Now he peeled off his gloves and let them drop to the ground.

With a nice straight stretch ahead, the tracks leading out of sight ahead, nothing visible, the guy gained confidence and sped up.

That's it, Zach urged him on. Nice path, no reason to think about the snow that had obviously fallen from branches ahead. His prey passed him, head not turning. One snowshoe passed over the first snare, but he was sloppy lifting the back foot.

It caught, sending the man stumbling forward. He swore sharply, but not in English. Russian wasn't one of Zach's languages, but he knew the profanities from it.

He launched himself before the white-clad man could regain his balance, hitting him hard. A guttural cry escaped the man as they crashed down, Zach's weight forcing the other man to the ground. Zach had the advantage from the beginning, since the man's feet were tangled with the snowshoes and he had to release the poles to free his hands.

He twisted frantically. Zach was ready, slamming a fist into that face. Despite the fleece covering, blood spouted from the nose hole. Zach kept hammering him. The guy was groping for something beneath his parka—a gun? a knife?—but Zach drove his knee onto that arm, hearing a snap, followed by a strangled scream that gurgled from the blood that must be filling his throat.

Zach locked his arm around the Russian's neck, wrenching back to gain complete control. Instead of submitting, the man fought viciously to dislodge Zach, making him think of a hooked trout flopping on the bank. He tightened the vee of his arm just as the man bucked with his entire body. Zach heard another snap. No, felt it.

Oh, damn, he thought, sickened. Not immediately releasing the hold, he bent to let the suddenly limp body sag onto the snow to one side of the trail. He stayed cautious, pressing his fingers to where the carotid artery in the neck should be pulsing and finding nothing.

Zach rose to his knees and stared down at a man he hadn't intended to kill if he could help it. He yanked up the balaclava, seeing the face of a stranger.

He'd really have liked to question this guy. Whatever his native language, he surely wouldn't have been chosen for this trek unless he spoke English with reasonable fluency.

Also…aware of a level of discomfort, Zach realized he had acclimated more to civilian society than he'd realized. He had started thinking like a cop, not a soldier fighting terrorists in lawless parts of the world. No, he couldn't have arrested this guy. He had no cuffs, no jurisdiction, but he could have tied him up, left him with whatever he needed to stay warm and sent the border patrol back to pick him up.

That wasn't happening.

An urgent voice in Zach's head said, *Get him out of sight. He can't be alone.*

He heeded it, setting aside the rifle and removing the pack from the man's back, then putting on his own snowshoes before dragging the dead man around the back of the cedar tree, well out of sight of the trail.

Then, feeling angry and unsettled, he hefted the rifle and pack behind the tree and did the same for the snowshoes and poles. They were intact, he was glad to see. He'd expected the bindings on the snowshoe, at least, to be damaged. The man had much larger feet than Ava did, but Zach was confident he could adapt these.

He returned to the trail and found a couple of new long growths of willow or alder, flexible enough to be bent to lie level with the ground, and secured them in place. He used the shovel to do his best to erase any sign that a struggle had taken place. After brushing snow over the top of the new snare, he took a few strategic steps in his own snowshoes, making it less obvious that one set of tracks had ended rather abruptly. Finally, he backed around the tree, erasing his own tracks as he went.

No, he didn't believe for a minute that this guy had been entirely on his own. More likely one had lagged, maybe because he'd investigated an animal track. Zach hoped the companion or companions hadn't been close enough to hear that scream.

He searched the body for weapons, appropriating a wicked knife and sheath, but found nothing else of interest. Then, pausing every thirty seconds or so to listen, he employed the shovel to dig a shallow grave in the snow, roll the body into it and cover it. A predator could dig it out with no effort, but at least it wasn't immediately obvious.

Zach knelt beside the bulging pack but paused for a moment to scan himself for new and old pain. Yeah, he'd felt the hard blow to his thigh, but it wasn't anything to worry about. His shoulder...wasn't happy. He swung his arm in a full circle. It was functional; all he could ask. His head throbbed, but his vision hadn't been impacted.

Then he started his search of the pack with the outside pockets. That's where he would stow additional weapons. Worse came to worst, he *was* armed now, but what he needed to employ was guerrilla warfare, which tended to be silent. Pulling the trigger of an automatic rifle amounted to jumping up and down and waving his arms.

Here I am! Come and get me!

The first and most accessible pocket held goggles and dark glasses. Both potentially useful.

He recognized the shape of what was inside the matching pocket on the other side even before he touched it. A handgun was noisy, too, but…

He lifted it out, a grin splitting his face. Zach was glad Ava couldn't see him right now; he probably looked more like a winter-starved wolf about to bring down a caribou than the kind of man she'd ever known.

But hot damn! This was an American-made pistol with a suppressor screwed onto the barrel. It was all his Christmases wrapped into one—a nearly silent, effective way to fight their way out of the trap this deep-cut valley increasingly felt like.

He could just shoot the next SOB who came down the trail.

The breath he let out scraped in his throat. No. He couldn't do that. He'd keep it handy, though, in case his catch and—not release— hold wasn't going to work. Or if he faced *two* opponents.

He had time to take a look inside the pack, pushing aside changes of clothes to see packets of freeze-dried meals—descriptions in English, all presumably purchased at a Canadian store that equipped hikers, climbers and skiers—and lots of loose candy bars. Matches, a stove—

Swish, swish, swish.

Body aching now, Zach wished he could just arrest the next creep, haul him to lockup and go home to a hot shower, a bowl of something comforting like chicken noodle soup and the chance to lie down on a comfortable mattress in the dark until he felt better.

Instead, he crouched again in his blind, let his gloves fall to the snow at his feet and waited.

At some point during the afternoon, Ava had lay down on her side and curled up, still clutching the sleeping bag around her, staring at the snow wall in front of her. Sitting up, keeping watch, wouldn't do her a speck of good, would it? What was she going to do, scrape her way out of this pit to attack one of those monsters with her bare hands?

Except they weren't bare, so she couldn't even use her fingernails. Which wouldn't be much use, anyway, because long, beautifully tended fingernails weren't compatible with her lifestyle.

She hadn't heard a single gunshot or voice. A snowshoe hare had hopped by, startling at the sight of her. More birds paused in branches high overhead. Once she did hear a piercing cry, as some small creature became prey. It sent a shock through her, because she felt as small, inconsequential and vulnerable as the mice and squirrels and chipmunks and hares that fed the larger predators.

The light was going, she began to realize, with a new chill of fear. Zach wouldn't wait until dark to return, would he? How would he find her?

Maybe he couldn't.

Would he dare call her name if he thought he was near?

God, she felt pathetic. She never, never wanted to be in this position again. It threw her back to that terrible time in her life when there'd been no safety anywhere for her, when *she* was the smallest, the most vulnerable.

She clenched her jaw. Zach said to wait, so that's what she'd do.

That was when she heard the swishing sound of someone approaching.

Ava strained, trying to decide which direction the person was approaching from, unable to be sure.

Whoever it was started coming directly *toward* her. Then Zach said softly, "Ava? Tell me you're here."

She let out an undignified whimper she prayed he didn't hear, and sat up. In an equally low voice that she thought came out remarkably calm, she said, "Where would I go? The mall?"

She heard his chuckle before she saw him, tall at the foot of the hole.

"We'll stay here tonight." He tossed a pair of snowshoes down and knelt to heave off a big pack. Two sets of poles followed the snowshoes, and then he lowered the pack, followed by—*gulp*—an automatic rifle.

That's when she really looked at him and saw his eyes. There was a wildness in them that made her shiver. He might sound completely self-possessed, but inside, he wasn't.

"You killed someone," she whispered.

The eyes flicked up and met hers. "Yes."

She swallowed and nodded, unable to chew him out, or not, or... What *could* she say?

Nothing.

"Let me wipe out my trail," he said, in that same, conversational tone. "Probably not necessary, but…" He vanished, and she transferred her gaze to his gleanings.

It finally registered that he had *two* sets of poles. Only one pack, but he couldn't carry more than one.

Unable to really even hear what he was doing, Ava just sat there until he reappeared, took off his snowshoes and jumped down into her hole.

"Are you okay? I was gone longer than I expected to be—"

She shook her head. "I'm—" Not bored. She hardly knew how to describe what she felt. "All right." Now she was.

He nodded and took a rolled sleeping bag from beneath stretchy bands at the top of the pack. A pad had been rolled up with it, she saw.

"You have two sets of poles." Ava hadn't even known she was going to say that.

"Yeah," he said gruffly. "I waited a long time to find out if anyone else would come along, but it appears only the two were sent on cleanup duty."

"Are they—"

"Both dead?" His eyes still didn't look right. "No. I…incapacitated the second man and left him tucked into his sleeping bag and tied up to a tree. We'll send someone back for him."

How did you "tuck" an unwilling man into a sleeping bag and then tie him up? Oh, duh—he must have been unconscious.

"I acquired quite a bit of food," he added. "Freeze-dried dinners and some desserts, too."

"Really?"

He smiled, and seemed to settle a little. "Our Russian terrorist had a sweet tooth."

Had. So he was the dead one.

"Are we really staying here for the night?"

"Where better?"

"I kept thinking—"

His eyebrows climbed.

"Well, that this looks an awful lot like a grave waiting for a coffin."

His head turned and he swore. "I'm sorry. That didn't occur to me."

At last, she could smile. "No, I shouldn't have said that. I had too long to think, that's all. Really, what could be cozier?"

Maybe he intended that sound to be a laugh.

"Shall I start dinner?"

"Yeah. I think we're safe here for the night. We probably don't want to break out in song, but I can't carry a tune, anyway, so that's just as well."

"Really?"

"Really. You?"

"I love to sing."

Now he openly grinned. "I love to listen."

Then they were a match made in heaven. Ava cringed, hoping he didn't read her thought.

She sat cross-legged and busied herself with her small cookstove. "These are my last dinners," she told him. "Pasta primavera. If you saw something better in there…" She nodded at the pack.

"I'm…not really hungry. Pick whatever you want."

She narrowed her eyes. "Why aren't you hungry?"

He opened his mouth, hesitated and then closed it. Thought better of lying to her? "I've…had a headache. Some nausea, too. Turns out extreme activity stirs it up."

"A concussion."

"Probably." He sounded amazingly unconcerned.

Mad, she said, "You didn't think to tell me this?"

Those eyes, not as expressionless as he probably imagined, met hers. "What could you have done?"

"We could have slowed down. Looked for a place to rest sooner! I could have—"

"No, Ava," he said, his voice both rough and gentle. "I'm not in that bad a shape. We have to follow the plan."

Frustrated, she wanted to keep arguing, but "should have" was pointless now, and she couldn't have set a snare, as he described it, bringing down the two armed men tracking them. He'd produced real snowshoes for her, food to sustain them and weapons she prayed she didn't have to use.

Her admiration for Zach swung higher, but she knew he didn't want to hear about it, and would shut down any attempt on her part to thank him.

Instead, she said, "Will you try to eat?"

One side of his mouth tipped up. "Okay. But make it pasta primavera. The ones I, er, acquired are store-bought. Which are better than MREs, but—"

She smiled, as he'd intended. Waiting for water to boil, she finally said, "Do you want to tell me about it?"

He seemed to be concentrating on the small flame. "Maybe after we eat."

How LITTLE COULD he get away with telling her?

Watching her as she prepared their meal, just as she had the previous night, he reconsidered his instinct to tell half-truths. No, she wasn't a soldier, but given her childhood, he suspected she wouldn't shock easily. They were in this together. He owed her the respect he'd have given any other teammate. What's more, the blunter he was, the more ready she'd be to pull that trigger if she had to.

He just hoped to God it didn't come down to that.

"You have a memory card in that camera?" he asked, nodding toward her pack.

"Yes, of course. Two different kinds. I've filled some."

"I want you to take out the most recent cards. We'll each carry one."

"Oh." She bent her head so he couldn't read her face well. "Yes, of course."

"Smells good," he offered. It did, and suddenly he was starved, too, but damn, what he craved most was stretching out in the sleeping bag and not moving for eight hours or more.

As they ate, they talked quietly. He told her a little about his current job as a detective for a rural county. "I like working independently," he said. "Using my head, figuring things out."

"Versus action?"

He grimaced. "Yeah. They wanted me on the SWAT team, but I said no. I used the excuse of my injury, but the truth is, I'm done with that."

"Except you're not."

"No." It was a minute before he added, "Lucky I haven't had time to get fat and lazy."

Ava laughed. "I just can't picture that."

He grinned. "You never know." The scrape of the spoon told him he'd eaten his entire serving. His stomach felt better enough, and he wondered if he'd mostly been hungry.

She talked about some of the outlets where she sold her work, telling him she had an agent, which was a good thing since she didn't have the right personality to do all the marketing herself. "Super outgoing and engaging isn't me. Of course," she said with a sigh, "I have to do a certain amount of it, anyway."

"You envision doing this forever?"

She set down the aluminum pan. "I know I can't. Once my knees go, you know…" When he smiled, she shrugged. "There are other types of jobs in the field. Sports, newspapers… I could sell prints of my work from an eBay shop."

If they stayed in touch—if they started something together—he was going to hate waving goodbye when she set off into the African bush or the jungles of Thailand or wherever the hell else she went to do her job. Except he guessed some of the time, maybe most of the time, she wouldn't be on her own. She'd have a guide, at least.

Okay, he could live with that. Except…what

he'd really like was to go with her. Carry, fetch, cook, watch her back.

And he was getting more than a little ahead of himself here.

He handed her his own dish and then dug in the pack he'd appropriated, producing a handful of candy bars. She pounced on a Twix; he went for Almond Joy and resisted having seconds when she did. Better be cautious.

Finally, watching her wiping out the dirty dishes with snow and stowing them away, he said, "I found passports."

Chapter Nine

Her head came up. "Real ones?" Her nose wrinkled. "You know what I mean."

"One was Russian, the other from Kazakhstan. The men flew into Montreal on different dates, close to two weeks ago. Both passports showed some previous travel, nothing likely to catch anyone's attention. Do I think those are their real names? No. When we get out of here, I'll give the passports to the border patrol."

"Do you think the man you left alive will survive until we make it out?"

He tried to keep his expression impassive. "Let's hope it doesn't take too long."

Her nod hid a lot, and he understood.

He talked more about the snares he'd set, and how well they'd worked on both occasions. "It helped that I had some height and weight on both of the men. That won't always be the case. I was also lucky because neither had a weapon in hand."

"Hard to use a pole if you're also clutching a gun."

He inclined his head. That would be a problem for him, too.

"There were eight men on that ridge?"

"No, I think seven. I can check for sure."

She twisted to take her camera out of her pack. What had to be a really expensive lens was obviously toast, but the camera itself came on for her. That had to be a super battery.

She brought up the photos again. She was right. Seven men. He took the camera from her and studied the three faces that she'd captured. None of those matched the two members of the group he'd taken down today.

"Five to go," he murmured. "And Borisyuk is one of them."

She didn't ask the obvious: Would the prime target expend his men before he got his own hands dirty, or would he enjoy killing two inconvenient Americans?

It was getting hard to see Ava's face, which Zach regretted. Even as tense as they both were right now, he liked seeing every flicker of her expressions.

"You brought your own sleeping bag," she said.

"You don't know how close I was to dumping it." He saw her startle. "I liked sleeping with you," he said wryly. "I'm afraid if I'm not, I'll wake up constantly, groping around to be sure you're there."

"We won't be far apart."

"I guess there's only so much space," he admitted, acknowledging the limited width of their hole.

She hadn't moved. He waited out her silence.

"We could…zip the sleeping bags together," she said softly.

WITH HER CHEEKS BURNING, Ava was grateful for the oncoming darkness. She also hoped he didn't take her invitation for more than she'd intended it to be. Sex wasn't casual for her. Truth be told, she'd never been able to relax enough, give enough of herself, for sex to be all that great—or, really, worth bothering with. She'd felt more intimacy sleeping in Zach's arms last night than she ever had when naked with any other man.

Maybe…

No. Don't even think it.

"I can go for that," he said calmly. "Shall we set up?"

"Yes." Woman of the world, that was her. "Then I suppose I'd better crawl out of here and, um, find some privacy."

"Ditto. Wait. You haven't stayed stuck in this

hole all day?" He was obviously frowning at her. "I didn't think…"

Could her face get any hotter? "No, I, um, used a plastic bag. Which I'll dump while I'm behind that tree."

He bent his head matter-of-factly. They took turns, Zach leaving the job of zipping the two sleeping bags together to what he described as her more nimble fingers.

He'd looked better over dinner than he had when he first appeared, but whatever good the meal had done him was already gone. His shoulders sagged. She caught him rubbing his temples when he didn't think she'd see. What bothered her most was seeing how…*still* he held himself. For a man who crackled with intensity, he seemed to have wound down.

She could not imagine that sex was on his mind.

Finally, in complete darkness he climbed into the sleeping bag, lay on his back with his head on a balled-up parka and waited while Ava slid in beside him.

She reached for his hand, which clasped hers firmly. "Are you okay?" she asked.

Long pause. "Been better," he admitted. "A night's sleep will do wonders."

She hoped so. If he looked this bad in the morning, she'd try to talk him into staying put where they were now that they wouldn't run out of food. She'd be even more strongly in favor of that if not for his injuries—the ones he'd told her about, and the ones he didn't want to admit to. He needed a hospital.

Also…would the terrorists, if that's what they were, really continue on their way minus their two compatriots? Or would they take the time to come looking for them—and for the problem they clearly hadn't solved?

Ava had a sick feeling that's exactly what they would do.

She'd have thought Zach had fallen asleep, except the hand holding hers hadn't relaxed. So she wasn't surprised when he spoke from the darkness.

"How are you?"

"Scared," she admitted. "Grateful."

He shifted. Turned his head to look at her? "For?"

"You," she said honestly. "I wouldn't have had a prayer alone. No, not just alone—even if I'd brought someone along on this trip. I've never met anyone like you."

"You must know some former soldiers."

"Yes, but…" They weren't warriors, but she wasn't sure he'd like that description. "You have different instincts, skills. How many people would know how to make snowshoes from some tree branches and a few cords? Would have the strength to go on when they were injured as badly as you were?"

"I'm okay—"

"You're not!" she said fiercely. "Don't lie to me!"

"Hey." His voice a gentle rumble, he rolled toward her enough to gather her up into his arms and settle her against his side. "I told you. I'm used to functioning with some pain. I'll bet you're a mass of bruises yourself, and you kept moving as long as you had to."

"It's not the same," she mumbled against his chest.

He seemed to be rubbing his cheek or jaw against her head. "Under the circumstances, my background has come in handy. You're right about that. I've faced worse odds and come out alive."

"But have you had to protect someone else?"

"Sure." He sounded surprised. "Locals in a bad spot, and my teammates, always. You…"

What felt like a hesitation drew out.

"Me what?"

"I…care about you. I'm not expecting anything from you, but if we'd met differently…" He huffed out a breath. "I need to keep you safe."

Her eyes stung. For an instant she listened

to his heartbeat. "I want *you* safe, too. I *hated* it when you left today, or thinking you'd sacrifice yourself."

His arms tightened. "I have faith you're capable of fighting if you have to."

Was he right? Ava tried to imagine how she could have brought down either of the men he'd surprised today, and knew she couldn't have done that. But could she pull the trigger of a gun to save his life, or hers? A hot coal of anger said, *Yes.*

"I just…want to say thank you. For being here."

"Which I wouldn't be if you hadn't dug me out of a snowy grave." That had to be a smile in his voice.

She sniffed, hoping he wouldn't hear, but something inside her relaxed, too. He was right. This partnership wasn't one-sided. She wasn't useless by any means.

"I got your arm back in the socket, too," she reminded him.

His chest vibrated with what had to be a laugh. "Yes, you did."

"Okay. Part of me wants to talk about tomorrow…"

"Let's wait until morning. I have some ideas, but I'll need to look at a map. Assuming you carried one?"

She bobbed her head. What she thought qualified as a hug followed. Really grateful she'd suggested they double up the sleeping bags, Ava concentrated on his warmth along her body, his heartbeat, his slow, deep breaths…and fell asleep.

ZACH'S EYES SNAPPED OPEN. Had he just shouted? His skin felt electrified, and he was desperate to jump to his feet, to be ready—

Taking in the silence but for the soft, rhythmic sound of Ava breathing, he made himself lie still. Damn, the nightmare had been a bad one; one of the worst. He'd been doing better, sleeping more peacefully.

Nothing like going to war again, killing, to stir up the muddy depths of a man's psyche.

He muttered a few foul words under his breath. Weirdly, except for the nightmare, he felt as if he were waking from a coma, no sense of time having passed. He'd been out until he was flung into an ugly moment of the past, and was now wide awake.

He became conscious that the night was exceptionally dark. Either cloud cover was heavy enough to hide the moon entirely, or the surrounding trees and high ridges did the same. After a long period of stillness, he didn't hear anything alarming. The wake-up call had been in his own head.

In fact, as he forced himself to relax, muscle by muscle, he realized that he was amazingly comfortable with Ava cuddled up to him. Her head still rested in the hollow of his shoulder beneath the collar bone, and their legs had come to be tangled.

He hadn't spent the night with a woman in so long, he could barely remember the last time. Since retiring, he hadn't even wanted sex enough to play the games required with a new partner. Apparently, he thought wryly, he was ready—except Ava wasn't the game-playing kind.

Because it was necessary, Zach ran the usual checklist: shoulder, not too bad, head still ached. How would he know if he was dizzy?

He slowly lifted his right arm and, without disturbing Ava, was able to punch the button on his watch to see that it was 3:00 a.m. Thank God his bladder didn't demand attention. He still had no desire to move. Lying here with an armful of woman suited him just fine. In the absence of another nightmare, he could get two or three more hours of sleep before dawn lightened the sky.

Not that they could get the same early start they had the past two mornings, he reminded himself. He'd have to tinker with the straps on the snowshoes to make them fit Ava's smaller feet. Then the two of them had to have a serious discussion about how they might evade Borisyuk and company.

His mind circled, not coming to any conclusions, until Ava mumbled something.

He bent his head. "Did you say something?"

"Quit worrying," she said drowsily. "I can hear you. Feel you. Something."

He smiled and pressed his lips to the top of her head. "Yes, ma'am."

She seemed to sink back to sleep immediately, and the exchange freed him to do the same.

Ava squirming to get out of the sleeping bag woke him come morning. In the gray light, he said, "What?"

"Have to pee."

"Oh." He lay back and enjoyed watching her wriggle into multiple layers of clothing, even though that meant she wouldn't be coming back to bed.

She grabbed something from her pack and scrambled up the bank, vanishing from his sight. With a groan, Zach pushed himself to sit up.

Damn. He felt even more battered than he had yesterday morning. His conditioning was sufficient for the traveling, but he hadn't needed two brutally physical fights, given his injuries. Curious, he lifted his fleece quarter-zip, along with the cotton tee beneath, and saw a motley collection of bruises that were a different color than the ones that lay beneath them. When he probed experimentally, he had to wonder if he didn't have a cracked rib or two, as well.

It wouldn't be the first time. He shrugged and winced. Good thing Ava hadn't seen that. He needed her to believe in him.

By the time she reappeared, he'd gotten dressed, too, not without wishing either of the men he'd tackled had been closer in size to him. He'd sure like a change of clothes. Standing, he groaned, wishing he'd had a chance to alleviate his stiffness.

"Oatmeal?" she asked.

"Sounds good." Boots on, he followed her path to the woods, and while he was there, he forced himself through some easy exercises to limber up his tight, aching muscles. The shoulder was improved today, he thought, despite what he'd put it through yesterday. The headache might have relented, too.

Neither talked much over breakfast. Ava kept sneaking looks at him he pretended not to notice. He suspected she was assessing his condition. He did the same in return, thinking that she'd visibly lost weight. They hadn't been eating enough, and both were probably getting dehydrated, too. The additional food and the second water bowl he'd acquired should help. He'd encourage her to drink more.

As she washed up the dishes and boiled water for what coffee she had left, he asked about her experience with firearms.

"I…did a little target shooting with a .22 rifle when I was a kid. It was fun, and I had a good eye, but that was a really long time ago. The target wasn't moving, and, well, it wasn't alive."

"No, you wouldn't have hunted," he acknowledged. She might be grateful right now for his capacity for violence, even the knowledge that he'd killed, but later, that might bother her. They weren't an obvious pairing.

He shook off more premature thoughts.

"I'm going to have you carry a handgun from here on out. I'll show you how to use it in principle, but even though the one I'm going to keep has a suppressor—a silencer—I'd just as soon not risk firing either gun."

"No! Oh, no."

He took out the Colt 9mm he'd lifted off his second victim, then showed her where the safety was and how to release it. He'd already verified that it was ready to fire, and that the magazine was full.

It was heavy for a woman's smaller hands, but she held it steadily, listening to his advice.

"Aim low. It'll kick up." He doubted the men hunting them wore any body armor. They were armed to the teeth, but hadn't really anticipated encountering anyone in the wilderness. If a helicopter had spotted them, they had come with the capability of shooting it down, which was different.

They must be cursing the chance that had led to them being spotted, and frustrated at not being positive the avalanche had taken the witnesses out. They couldn't realistically have expected the two scouts to rejoin them yet, not when they'd been ordered to take a lengthy detour. That said… Zach and Ava had lost most of a day after the avalanche hit, and then another full day when he went back to deal with the pair of hunters.

The question now was whether the main body of the group would simply wait there, or whether they'd proceed north again to pick up the two missing members, and potentially any survivors of the avalanche.

Before he started on the snowshoes, he asked for any maps she had, and they pored over the one she produced.

"Where were you dropped?" he asked.

She tapped a marked campsite.

His finger traced the length of the trail to roughly where the avalanche had caught them. "I was set down farther upriver, since I intended the trip to last no more than a week."

Ava looked rueful. "I was about to turn back. Just think, if I had before I set eyes on those men…"

"If you'd snowshoed downriver with no detours, you might have met up with them there."

She made a face. "I wonder what would have happened if I'd been able to call for a national park helicopter and they'd heard it coming."

Rather than reacting to that, he frowned at her. "Why *didn't* you turn back, if it was already on your mind?"

"I'm embarrassed to say it was because I suddenly realized someone was behind me."

"So you were running away from me." In other words, her involvement was his fault, one hundred percent. If she'd turned back that morning, he'd probably have exchanged a few polite words with her, then continued northward—and likely been alone when he saw the heavily armed group above. The binoculars he'd carried were fine, but he doubted he would have been able to pick out Borisyuk's face.

"I…suppose so. Except, it had long since

become obvious you were gaining ground on me." She looked perturbed. "I don't really know what I was thinking."

If not for the camera, would the terrorists have bothered to try to bury Zach under an avalanche? He didn't know, but if they had, at least Ava would have been safely going on her way, unaware of what she'd missed.

And he'd be dead, assuming he was in the same place at the same time.

Which was unlikely. Chances were better he'd have been deep in tree cover and unable to see the ridgetop on one side or the mountains on the other. He'd have enjoyed his trip, maybe wondered about the beautiful woman snowshoeing on her own out here—and Borisyuk would be passing unobserved through the wilderness, close to a planned pickup point.

He shouldn't regret anything, if there was the slightest chance they could stop that bastard. And yet, he did. He'd give damn near anything, including his life, to know that Ava was safe, even if that meant he had never had a chance to sleep with her pressed against him, her head on his shoulder.

Damn it.

Chapter Ten

"There are several trails turning off when we get closer to the end of this one," he said, tapping them with his finger.

"Yes, but one is where hikers on the ridge will emerge from—"

He conceded that with a nod.

"And this trail dead-ends at a lake." Her fingertip almost touched his. "I'm assuming they have this map, or a comparable one." Too bad the men weren't traveling aimlessly, but they were too well equipped not to have a compass and maps.

Zach told Ava what he was thinking. "There are a couple of possible alternatives. One is that, if we see tracks descending the ridge trail, we head up it." Assuming he and she made it that far.

She looked at him in surprise. "They'll just let us stroll by?"

He grimaced. "Not unless I can eliminate

whoever was left on guard there. If they plan well, the rest of them will be spread out across all the possibilities."

Emotion flared in her eyes. "I hate it when you say things like that."

"Eliminate?"

"Yes!"

"We're now either victims or victors," he said bluntly. "I don't know about you, but I want to be able to—" *Go home.* That's what he'd almost said. A picture crossed his mind of the small rambler on an acre he was currently renting while he decided whether to stay in the Bellingham area or not. Home? No, it was a place to lay down his head, no different than base housing. Funny time to realize what he *wanted* was a real home that included a family.

She was staring at him. Waiting for him to finish.

"I want to be able to get *you* home safely," he concluded.

"Home," Ava echoed, in an odd tone. Then she sighed. "Okay, what looks like the best bet to you?"

"We either head out cross-country—there are a couple of possible creeks—or think about the trail that climbs over this pass." He touched his fingertip to the map. "The zigzag line suggests it's steep, but it has to be doable. I wonder if the snow isn't year-round up there. Hikers and mountain climbers obviously navigate it. And once we get high enough, we'll have a better chance of cell phone coverage."

Her gaze met his again. "They'll surely be watching that route."

"Yeah. But all of them?"

Divided they fall. And he *was* armed now.

"There's not really a choice, is there?"

"No. Unless—keep checking your cell phone."

"Did either of them carry phones?"

"Both, but they're the cheap ones you pick up at the pharmacy. Who's your carrier?" When she told him, he nodded. "I'm betting you have better coverage."

"Okay."

Fortunately, one of the many smart decisions she'd made was to bring a couple of portable chargers. Her phone wouldn't run out of juice.

Except for a few necessary words, neither said anything else while she packed up and he worked on the bindings of her newly appropriated snowshoes.

Once he had her try them on, she offered him a crooked smile. "I deeply appreciate the expertise that allowed you to make my existing snowshoes. Really. But I'll still be thrilled to toss them into the woods."

Zach laughed. What he didn't say was that they wouldn't have dared take on what had to be a difficult climb to the pass if he hadn't been able to provide a replacement for the flimsy snowshoes that were already breaking apart.

Just before they set out, he changed into a white parka, even though it was a tighter fit than he liked, and utilized the white tarp to fling over the heavy pack. Ava looked alarmed, but only nodded when he said, "It'll give them pause at first sight."

As they beat their way back to the trail, Zach adjusting again to the weight of the pack, he couldn't prevent himself from running his own calculations, over and over. If the five remaining men continued on the ridge trail until its natural end, down at some other creek—if memory served—how long would it take them to head back up the valley, realize the two men sent on a separate errand should have appeared, and then figure out where he and Ava had gone?

What would he do if they came around a curve and found themselves face-to-face with any or all of the men?

Reaching the trail, completely untracked as it continued southward, Ava said unexpectedly, "We can worry ourselves in circles without helping."

How did this woman read his mind? "You're right," he said shortly, but planted a pole to free his hand long enough to pat the pistol he carried in the pocket of the parka, then reached back to estimate how long it would take him to get the automatic rifle in position to spray bullets.

ZACH INSISTED ON taking the lead, she presumed because of what he wore. The sight of that familiar parka and fur-lined hood might provide a critical couple of seconds before they realized he was a stranger.

Please.

It took her a few minutes to adjust to wearing the less cumbersome, modern snowshoes again, as well as having real poles, but after that she marveled at how fast they were now able to move. If Zach was being hindered by his shoulder injury or headache, she couldn't tell. A couple of times he opened enough of a lead on her that he paused after glancing over his shoulder so she could catch up. She didn't let herself feel chagrined. He was bigger, stronger and longer legged. After all, he'd gained fast on her even that first day. Still, Ava felt confident she wasn't holding him up much.

There weren't a lot of distinctive landmarks along this stretch. One small creek—mostly ice choked—crossed the trail. She poked with the tip of her pole at some ice and was surprised when it didn't so much break up as disintegrate. That was the moment when she became aware that she was too warm.

"Hold up," she called in a low voice.

Zach stopped and deftly turned his snowshoes so he could raise his eyebrows at her.

"It's warming up," she said.

He frowned, taking in the many snow-laden branches to each side of the trail. "Snow's not melting yet."

"No, but almost."

He pushed back the hood, as if testing the temperature. "That could be good or bad," he said thoughtfully.

Ava knew what he meant. A sudden melt would turn the trail into a slushy mess and expose whatever growth had happened since park personnel or volunteers had cut it back. Probably a brief warming wouldn't extend long; the park wouldn't really open to hikers until July. But she and Zach were at a relatively low elevation here, at the bottom of the valley.

"I'm going to take my parka off." She stripped off her gloves and unzipped, aware Zach was evaluating what she wore beneath. No, her next layer, a fleece quarter-zip, was not bright red, so she ignored his scrutiny but saw that he wasn't following suit. Of course not; that white parka with the hood was a disguise. Once she stashed her parka beneath an elastic strap, she pulled on her gloves again and said, "I'm ready."

His eyes lingered on her for a moment that felt…personal. Even warm. But abruptly he turned and set off again, Ava falling in behind him.

If we get out of this, I'll probably never see him again, she reminded herself, but discovered that she didn't actually believe that. Given what he'd said, would he let her go that easily? Would she go without making some effort to find out whether he might be interested in—

What? Spending a couple of nights together?

Ava was disconcerted to realize she'd take even that. She wanted to keep sleeping with him, and more.

The sound of something thrashing through the thick vegetation snapped her back to the present, and she came to a stop behind Zach, who'd raised one hand to signal her. A deer stepped out into the open in front of them, saw them, and took a giant leap into the tangled growth on the other side of the trail, going toward the river.

"She didn't expect us," he murmured, and resumed his long, easy stride.

An hour later, they had another unexpected encounter with wildlife. Zach stopped and said quietly, "Look."

A wolf stood so still beneath the branches of a cedar, his golden eyes on them, they might almost have passed without seeing him at all. Ava longed for her camera, packed away with the damaged lens. Reclusive creatures, gray wolves didn't show themselves any more often than did the lynx she'd hoped to see. She'd heard howling, but in the far distance. Now he evaluated them, then melted out of sight without making a sound.

"Suggests he hasn't met any other people recently," Zach said softly.

That was a heartening thought.

They made swift progress, finally stopping for a bite to eat beneath an old cedar tree much like the one the wolf had used for cover.

Ava was glad to shrug out of the pack for a few minutes. She felt stronger today, though, and it wasn't just the new-and-improved snow-shoes. The avalanche had been…she had to think. Three days ago? Yes. Three nights had intervened. Her aches and pains were fading. She hadn't been able to see her face, but guessed the visible bruises were, too.

As Zach spilled some raisins into the palm of his bare hand, she studied him. His face was thinner, she felt sure, maybe even gaunt, although with the brown scruff that was swiftly becoming a short beard, it was hard to be sure. She'd noticed earlier without paying attention that he had dark bruises beneath both eyes. Not quite black eyes, but close. Now the almost purple color was muddied by some yellow. The lines carving his forehead seemed deeper, too, if she wasn't mistaken.

He'd moved today with the strength, grace and certainty that she'd seen when he first appeared behind her, but that had to be deceptive. He seemed determined to hide his pain, which might have offended her, except she guessed soldiers in the kind of unit he'd belonged to were always reluctant to show weakness. The fact that she was a woman might have nothing to do with his determination to disguise any vulnerability.

Or maybe he wasn't thinking about it at all; maybe he was utterly focused on what lay ahead of them. What he still had to do.

Yes, she thought. That's the kind of man he was.

He was looking right back at her, she suddenly realized, one of his unusually mobile eyebrows quirked. "Deep thoughts?"

"No, just thinking you look leaner. I suppose I've lost weight, too."

"Easily regained," he said lightly. "You ready to get going again?"

"Of course." Turning her face from his, she tucked the remnants of her snack—or was this lunch?—back into a pocket of her pack. While she was thinking about it, she took out her phone.

At his raised brows, she had to shake her head.

Shortly after they set out again, Ava realized the trail was climbing slightly to proceed higher above the level of the river. It now cut across a side hill. Although much of the undergrowth—the salal and gooseberry, the Oregon grape and lower clumps of devil's club—were mostly buried under snow, the trail here squeezed between a heavy growth of trees, the ubiquitous cedar, hemlock and spruce mixed with more deciduous ones than she'd noticed farther up the valley. She thought she recognized maples, even without any hint of budding leaves. She seemed to remember that dogwood was common, too, as well as aspen and the every-present alder and willow.

Zach had slowed down somewhat, although she didn't see any awkwardness in his stride or the way he planted his poles. He might be watching more carefully. He wouldn't like not being able to see far ahead, she knew, given the density of the forest, as well as the curve of the trail. She tried harder to listen, too, but was afraid she wouldn't hear an approaching snow-shoer over the *swish-swish* of their own steps.

"I think I see a sign sticking out of the snow," he told her over his shoulder, voice barely audible.

She hadn't come from this far south, but of course national park employees would mark trails.

"Wait," Zach said sharply, but still quietly. "There are tracks on it."

Oh, God. Ava froze between one step and the next.

Then a voice called what sounded like an inquiry…in a harsh language she didn't recognize.

ZACH HAD REHEARSED for this moment since they started out this morning. With his hands encased in thick winter gloves, he couldn't get his index finger in to squeeze the trigger on the handgun he carried in the pocket at his hip. Given the warming temperatures, he considered leaving off his right glove, but the day still hovered around freezing, and he didn't dare let his fingers get numb or stiff. So he'd practiced, over and over.

Yank hand from the glove, leave it hanging

from his pole. Reach the short distance, take gun from the pocket.

He'd left the safety off to eliminate the one step.

He had run through it over and over in his mind, and practiced ditching the glove and reaching for the butt of the gun a dozen times. Either Ava was concentrating intensely on maintaining her pace, or giving what attention she had left over to watching and listening for company, but she showed no indication she'd noticed what he was doing or why.

Now, when the white-clad snowshoer appeared not fifteen yards ahead, Zach pulled the gun within three to four seconds.

The greeting, initially friendly sounding, gave him the time he needed. With five or six days' worth of scruff covering half his face and sunglasses over his eyes, Zach couldn't look that different at first glance from this guy's compatriots.

But when Zach didn't respond immediately, there was a gradual shift in body language and expression. The gaze slid past Zach, took in Ava.

This enemy's hand moved swiftly to the firing mechanism of the sniper-type rifle he carried slung over his shoulder, barrel pointing forward. Toward Zach and Ava.

Zach dropped his poles and braced his own gun in a two-handed firing position. With the suppressor screwed to the barrel, it was more awkward than what he was used to, but from this distance—

"I'm an American police officer," he said loudly, clearly. "Put down your weapons. *Now!*"

The man lifted the rifle, and Zach swore he was pointing it at Ava.

Zach fired, even as the man facing him did the same. Behind him, Ava cried out and either went down or flung herself to one side. He couldn't afford to turn.

He pulled the trigger three times, stopping only as he saw the white-clad figure folding in on itself, tumbling to the snowy ground. Zach had seen death take enough people to recognize it on this man's face. Still, he raced forward, yanked the rifle away from his adversary, and then spun clumsily and scrambled back to Ava.

Who, thank God, was picking herself back up. "He tried to shoot me," she whispered. "I think he *did* shoot me."

"What?"

"My arm stings, that's all, and—" She reached up to finger a tear in her parka on her upper arm.

"God." He fell to his knees beside her. "You scared me."

"*I* scared you?"

"*He* scared me." Zach had a bad feeling he was shaking, but he couldn't let himself yank her into his arms. The seasoned soldier he was had begun scanning for any indication of company before he'd even pulled the trigger. He wished he hadn't felt obligated to give a warning. He'd been desperate to prevent the other man from firing.

His brain was already turning that over when Ava said, "I didn't hear his gun go off. Or yours. Well, except for a few pops."

"You're really all right?" he demanded to know.

Her eyes were wide, shocked, but as always, determined. "Yes."

"Let me see," he insisted.

Wincing, she eased her arm out of the parka, and he was able to push aside the torn fabric of her fleece top and the turtleneck she wore beneath it to see a graze. Blood seeped, but treating it could wait. An inch or two to the left, and they'd be dealing with a real wound. Conceivably a shattered bone.

Heart racing from the close call, his thoughts jumped back to her comment about hearing only a few pops.

Galvanized by his realization, Zach pushed himself to his feet and returned to the rifle that lay where he'd tossed it, sunken in snow. He picked it up, astonished. Yes, it, too, had been fitted to fire silently. The AK-47s the other two had carried hadn't been; he wasn't even sure they *could* be. The shooter had to practice to achieve accuracy with the addition to any of the military's various sniper rifles, but they could be and sometimes were fitted with suppressors. There were moments when you had to go in quiet.

Zach couldn't believe his luck. He hadn't been primarily a sniper, but he'd gone through training at Fort Bennett and had utilized his skills plenty of times. He might still have qualms about picking off the remaining members of the terrorist group like ducks in a shooting gallery, but the fact that this man's first instinct on seeing Zach and Ava had been to gun them down sent a strong message.

"He's…dead?" she asked from behind him.

"Yeah. It was him or us."

"I saw." She'd stayed on the trail but advanced to within a few feet of the man. "What do we do with him? And which way do we go?"

God, he could love this woman, tough enough

to pass through terror into practicality and grit within a minute or two.

Maybe he already did.

This wasn't the time to become mired in the sinkhole created by emotions.

He still didn't hear any indication of other people nearby. They had to have spread out, the way he'd both feared and hoped.

That didn't mean he and Ava could afford to waste a minute.

He slung the rifle over his shoulder, straightened and looked around. "Get him out of sight, for starters." He evaluated the tracks. "Don't know how far he went up this trail before he decided we couldn't possibly be ahead of him and turned to come back. Maybe all he was doing was rejoining the main trail, but he might have been ordered to hang back out of sight, to lie in wait for us. Somehow, we surprised him."

"He certainly surprised *me*," she said dryly.

Zach spared a glance at her face, to see that for all her outward gutsiness, it was pinched. This was likely the only violent death she'd ever seen—unless at some point during that year while she'd tried as a seven-year-old to survive on the streets, she'd seen someone stabbed or shot. It was all too possible. He'd have to ask her what city she'd been in.

"Okay," he said. "You're going to stand guard while I carry his body back to the main trail and look for a good place to dump him. Then I'll get rid of his pack and snowshoes, too."

"Rifle?"

"That, we're keeping. In fact—"

To her obvious consternation, he gave her a one minute short course in firing a McMillan TAC-50, a sniper rifle used by Canadian military as well as by other countries. Zach had never personally fired one, but it made sense these guys had been able to get their hands on one on the black market.

Fortunately, for these purposes, she could ignore the scope. All she needed to do was point and fire. She wouldn't be shooting anyone from more than twenty, twenty-five yards, tops.

Ava did not look thrilled, but finally nodded, her teeth sinking into her lower lip. "Just… hurry, okay?"

Hanging around here at the junction of two trails was dangerous. "Yeah."

It took only a matter of minutes for him to drop his own pack, strip off the dead man's and heave the body over his right shoulder. Feeling the strain and the pain on the injured side of his body, he grunted. The guy was no lightweight, and Zach hoped he wouldn't have to go far to find the right spot.

He turned back the way he and Ava had come, and hadn't gone thirty feet before he noticed a particularly thick tangle of vegetation. He strode as close to it as he could, trying not to break branches, and did his best to fling a body that had to weigh 180 pounds or so. To his gratification, it disappeared.

He hustled back, seeing that Ava appeared frozen in place but still held the rifle in firing position, and crouched to conduct a cursory search of the pack. Another passport, this one from Uzbekistan. He pocketed that. Otherwise, the only thing worth holding on to was a handgun with a suppressor. He switched it out for the 9mm he'd given Ava earlier, then hauled the pack down the trail and threw it next to the body.

He took a few minutes to try to erase tracks, grimacing at his mixed success, and then smoothed over signs of the violent confrontation as best he could.

Finally, since no one else had appeared and he didn't hear any indication of someone close by, he gently took the rifle back from Ava and pulled her into his arms.

Chapter Eleven

Ava didn't know why she felt so traumatized now, after all the horrifying events of the last four days, but heaven help her, she might as well be a quaking aspen in a stiff breeze. She did a lot more than lean on Zach; she wrapped her arms around his torso, buried her face in his parka-clad shoulder and hung on for all she was worth. And shook.

He was talking, or only growling things under his breath. She couldn't make out a word he said. It had to be a couple of minutes before she realized she wasn't the only one shaking. The cold, bare hand that smoothed hair from her face definitely had a tremor. She rubbed her cheek against it, hard, and wished they were done, that this was the end and they could just stand here in each other's arms for the next half an hour or so.

But fear still squeezed her heart, and at last she lifted her head to look up at him. Eyes espresso dark met hers, and he said something else, still imperceptible. Then he wrapped her jaw with one hand, lifted her chin and kissed her.

This was like the other time, but more. He demonstrated with his mouth and teeth and tongue how desperate he felt, how hungry. Scared, too, she thought. *Like me.*

He all but devoured her, except she responded with equal ferocity. She *needed* this. Him. Her mind blurred, until she quit thinking, only wanted.

But then, with a gut-wrenching groan, he tore his mouth from hers. His eyes burned into hers. "Damn, Ava. You have no idea—" He bit off the rest, as if she couldn't guess what he hadn't said. His hand still shook, if for another reason now, when he stroked her face, as if that touch was precious.

Only, he straightened after that, and she had to loosen her grip on him and do the same.

"We have to get moving," he said gruffly.

She swallowed and squared her shoulders. "I know. I just—"

"This trail leads to the lake. I think we have to take it and then set out cross-country. I hope to God that's even possible."

She couldn't think, not without looking away from his intensity. "There's only the one track leading this way," she heard herself say.

"Yeah."

"But if he's already made it here, the others…"

"Must have divvied up the alternatives."

"Except, he thought you were one of his buddies."

"Momentarily, yeah. Maybe he assumed a teammate had cut back to report a sighting. Still, they wouldn't have split up and started investigating alternate routes the way it appears they've done if they'd hadn't started to worry. Even so, they're probably still pretty confident. For good reason. You and I haven't moved very fast, between the twenty hours or so before we were able to set off at all, and the slow pace because of your primitive snowshoes." He grimaced. "And my condition."

"So the rest of them have been expecting the two sent off to make sure no witnesses survived to zip along by now, or at least any minute, and say, 'No problem.'"

His mouth quirked. "Probably in another language, but yeah." His grimness returned. "Three down, four to go."

Her stomach rolled. "If they gang up on us—"

"We're still in deep trouble," he agreed. "I'd like to avoid that happening. And unfortunately—" he lifted his arm and checked his watch "—we've lost a lot of this day. If you're up to it, we should still keep going for a few hours, but that won't get us much past the lake, if at all."

"If only we'd searched harder for your pack. I'm sorry."

How many times had they had this discussion? The satellite radio he'd carried would have brought help within hours. If only *she'd* been smart enough to carry one, too—

"Knock it off," he said roughly. "We searched as long as we dared. It was miracle enough that you found *me*."

What more was there to say? Ava only nodded, taking in the sight of a man who looked as battered as she felt, yet also dangerous and still strong. His lips were a little swollen and had cracked. Averting her face, she licked her own and tasted blood.

Oh.

She felt his gaze on her face, and there was a discernible pause before he stepped away. He slung his pack on his back again, and the rifle over his shoulder. She saw him pat the right pocket of his parka where he carried the handgun, pull on his gloves and grip his poles.

"You lead," he said, moving aside.

Well, at least someone had broken the trail for her already. She set off briskly.

THE TRACKS THEY followed ended fifteen minutes later, where the latest dead man had turned around to go back. The unbroken snow slowed them down a little, since it wasn't always clear what was trail beneath the snow and what wasn't. They were left to flounder a few times before backing up and trying again.

Their next break, Zach and Ava studied the contour map again. That itch aggravated his spine constantly now, but however much he'd have preferred an alternative, it still looked like their best bet of cutting over to the ridge trail was from the lake, nestled in a high bowl. A fold of land lay between the two trails—not a high ridge, but steep on this side and forested. To his regret, with the sky high and blue, there was no possibility of another convenient, late-spring snowstorm to help them disappear.

That probably would have been asking for too much.

He turned so frequently to watch behind them, he'd have whiplash by the time they stopped for the night. He didn't dare miss anything, though. Any faint sign of a pursuer, he'd send Ava on ahead and set up himself with the rifle. He didn't need a snare this time; he could kill long-distance.

Not for the first time, he wondered how law enforcement would judge his choices, but he was damned if he'd second-guess them. Everything that mattered to him was on the line here: bringing Ava, an innocent civilian and a woman he could love, to safety; stopping a threat to the nation he'd spent ten years of his life fighting to protect; and, probably in last place but still meaningful, his own survival. He'd hoped never to kill again, but he intended to do whatever proved necessary to protect what mattered to him.

He paused where he had a decent sight line to the trail behind him between tall trees and scanned with binoculars. Still nothing. Where were the others? In the next hour or two, they'd know for sure that they had a major problem on their hands. Zach had to circle back to wondering what Borisyuk was thinking. Shouldn't his mission be at the forefront? He'd lost some men; Zach doubted this cold-blooded terrorist gave a damn. He was still in a position to get the hell out of this wilderness and on his way to the job awaiting him. Why *wouldn't* that be his choice?

He could have gone on with only, say, one of the men, leaving the others to clean up behind him. If that was the case, he might still be able to wreak havoc that could be devastating for this country. But he also risked having one or more of those men captured and, potentially, talking.

Zach hummed in his throat. If these were all dedicated terrorists, Borisyuk might believe he was safe from betrayal no matter what. If they were mercenaries hired to get him across the border, though…that was different. Did those men even know who he was?

When he wasn't snatching looks over his shoulder, Zach rarely took his eyes off Ava, which was distracting in its own way. Hard not to let his gaze linger on her long, strong legs and taut butt outlined in stretchy fabric. To picture her face, and aching at the memory of her passionate response to his kiss.

That wasn't what he should be thinking about now, though. Protecting *her* was too much of what mattered. In a way, she represented all the other Americans who would suffer if a terrorist accomplished his goal.

The psychology of his opponents, and particularly their leader, played in Zach's mind as he climbed the trail rising above the deepest cut of the river, following a creek that murmured in the background of his consciousness, but only made a sparkling appearance from snow cover and ice to tumble in mini waterfalls on occasion.

What Zach thought was that Borisyuk had an ego problem. Maybe he'd set out on his deadly path years ago with complete dedication to a twisted ideal, but he'd been too successful. He'd become a legend, and he *couldn't* let himself run like a frightened rabbit. He would not, could not, let himself believe he could be outmaneuvered, refused to believe anyone was smarter or more capable than him. Maybe it wasn't even the possibility of a photograph that still drove him. Once he realized three of his men had failed to stop whoever had survived the avalanche, his determination would harden. One or two people, mere backcountry travelers? Inconceivable!

At this moment, he probably still felt smug. One of his men would show up with evidence of the death of any Americans foolish enough to get in his way. But that smugness would wane as time passed. Eventually, he'd send someone to venture back up the trail, where the snowshoe tracks would initially be confusing, but eventually make clear that three people had met up—and only two of them had gone on.

No, Borisyuk wouldn't be prepared to quit, to say, "A photograph of me? What does that matter?"

Of course Zach couldn't be certain, but he thought he was right. And *that* was both good and bad. Good because it meant he and Ava still had a chance to kill or capture an infamous terrorist. Bad because they were still in great danger.

The trail broke into the open, and Zach paused to lift binoculars to his eyes and scrutinize the land below him. Still nothing, but that might only be because the dense Northwest rainforest hid so much.

Another hour passed, and the two of them paused for a drink and a handful of nuts. At Ava's worried look, he shook his head. They didn't talk at all, only went on. Two hours, three. The sun was dropping in the sky. In another couple of hours, it would go behind the mountains, and they'd lose light fast. They needed to take refuge soon. Not generally an optimist, he thought maybe he'd been expecting pursuit sooner than it could reasonably occur. The lake couldn't be far—not that it offered any safety.

His eye was caught by multiple deer tracks diverting from the trail. He'd seen them off and on all day, sometimes going off into the forest. This was different. It looked like a favorite route for the four-footed residents of these mountains. And, damn—that almost had to be a track left by a bear. Or Bigfoot.

"You seeing deer tracks up there?" he called.

Ava stopped and looked back. "Yes. I can see the lake, too. The ice is breaking up."

"Come here and tell me what you think."

She lifted her snowshoes in a quick turn and returned to his side.

He pointed with his pole. "Animal trail."

"Going the way we want to go."

"That's what I'm thinking."

"I say we take a chance." Her eyes widened. "Is that a bear track?"

"Has to be." His mouth quirked. "Probably just woke up. Can't be in a good mood."

Ava made a face at him. "Thank you for that. Do you want me to go ahead again?"

"Yeah, I'm going to try to muddy the tracks a little."

She nodded and set off. Looked like they'd face a steeper climb now.

Zach tramped all the way to the lake, made a mess in the snow then turned back. He went a little past the animal trail, snapped off a branch, swung around again and started swiping behind him as he moved backward. He did the same for ten yards or so onto the alternate trail, but going backward uphill was a strain, so he abandoned the effort. His best hope was that a few more animals would travel this way as the day waned—and maybe some nocturnal creatures, too. Someone hunting humans might not pay attention to the deer, rabbit and raccoon tracks that they'd been seeing everywhere.

Zach didn't relax his watchfulness any as he turned and sped after Ava.

AVA'S THIGHS BURNED. The trail meandered in a way one cleared and leveled by humans didn't. It turned out deer didn't think a thing of bounding straight upward, too. She had to pause every ten minutes or so, breathe deeply and wait for her muscles to relax. It was like doing sprints in training, she consoled herself; short, fast sprints divided by brief rests.

She hated that, when she caught a glimpse of Zach behind her, she couldn't read his expression at all, beyond obvious grimness. It was as if he'd pulled inside somewhere. His gaze didn't meet hers; his eyes were dark and curiously flat. He moved steadily but for his regular stops to search the landscape behind them. His head would tilt, and she had a suspicion he had better hearing than she did.

She hoped he did; she was depending entirely on him right now.

She didn't descend into the kind of exhaustion she had in previous days, when she couldn't think about anything but which foot to move next. *Gee, I've gained some conditioning*, she thought. But really, it was more the shock and fear of the earlier encounter sending her adrenaline into overdrive, and she still felt it circulating in her blood.

The speed with which the incident had erupted stunned her. Very few words exchanged, a gun barrel swinging toward her, the weird, compressed sound of silenced guns and the sting as a bullet creased her arm. The body collapsing, the *look* in his eyes—

Ignoring the momentary queasiness, she reminded herself to wash and bandage the still stinging place on her upper arm. She felt sure Zach wouldn't have forgotten.

The track curved to level out briefly, although they hadn't reached the top of the ridge. Just as it curved back and began to climb again, bear tracks continued straight. She had bigger things to worry about, but still exhaled with relief. She'd be just as glad not to stumble on an irritable, hungry bear.

Maybe he had a cave up here, it occurred to her. He might be like the famous groundhog; he or she had emerged to decide whether winter was past, and thought, *Nah. I'm going back to bed.*

A strange sound came to her ears. She froze between one stride and the next, trying to identify it. Zach exploded into action, catching up to her with shocking speed.

"That's somebody behind us. Don't know if there are two of them, or whether he stumbled, cracked his shin and swore, but that was a voice."

She clenched her teeth to be sure they couldn't chatter. When she was confident she wouldn't give away her panic, she asked, "What do we do?"

"Go on until we find a place I can set up," he said tersely. For the first time in the past couple of hours, she felt as if he was seeing *her*, and his expression was raw. "If I can hide you and my pack, I may climb a tree."

She bobbed her head. "You go ahead, then. You know what you're looking for."

Without another word, he passed her and set off fast, despite the crosshatch technique needed to climb in snowshoes. She did her best to keep up. The worst part was that she didn't hear so much as a whisper of sound behind her. It made her picture a little red dot centered on the back of her head. One pull of the trigger—

Go, go, go.

"Here," Zach said suddenly.

They weren't at a high enough elevation for the trees to be stunted yet. He seemed to have his eye on a cluster of big hemlock or Douglas fir, she wasn't sure, probably spruce and certainly cedar. The snow cover thinned to almost nothing beneath the spreading branches.

He pointed. "Get under cover, well back. Hunker down. Have your handgun ready to fire. Do you understand?"

"Yes. Yes."

He didn't move until she took a couple of

steps, then removed her snowshoes and kept going on the side hill, a foot slipping here and there, but she caught herself with a hand on the branches and rough trunks.

When she glanced back, she couldn't see Zach anymore. That scared her, but she had to trust that he knew what he was doing. Of course he did.

Finally, she crawled beneath a cedar tree. The feathery branches brushed the ground. Ava had to push them aside. With shuddering relief, she dropped the poles and snowshoes, eased off her pack and dug the gun she didn't even like to handle out of the outside pocket.

Then she crawled to a position where she could just see traces of her own tracks between the thankfully lush branches that she hoped would still hide her. She decided to sit up; a lot of positions would be hard to sustain for long. Then she took off her right glove, as Zach had taught her, pushed the tiny button to turn off the safety and listened to herself breathe. She just couldn't let herself get so scared that she accidentally shot Zach.

No. I have to wait to make sure.

MUCH LIKE HE'D done setting up the previous ambushes, Zach continued on ten yards until the trail curved enough that a pursuer was unlikely to notice that one of the two people ahead had peeled off. He'd see only tracks heading on.

Then Zach stepped carefully off the trail and circled back to his chosen trees. He stashed his pack and equipment out of sight and, with the rifle slung over his shoulder, started to climb.

This was an old enough cedar to have branches he hoped would hold his weight. If he could get high enough, he'd be able to step over to a spruce that would give him a better sight line down the trail. He'd kept his gloves on to give himself a good grip. If a branch broke and he fell, they were screwed.

Each scramble upward was made gingerly. He tested some of his weight on a branch, then all of it, but kept an arm around the trunk or a hand gripping the limb above to keep himself from plummeting.

He still didn't hear anybody approaching, but knew he couldn't be mistaken.

At last, maybe twenty-five feet off the ground, he found a perch that felt secure and gave him a hell of a view.

He was planning to kill in cold blood. He couldn't issue a warning, not when this SOB was likely carrying a fully automatic weapon that could spray bullets to cut him down along with half of this stretch of forest, too.

The shot wouldn't be long, which was just as well since he hadn't practiced at the range at more than two hundred yards since he got out of the service. The old skills were probably there, but he was just as glad not to have to test them. If all went well, this shot wouldn't even be a hundred yards.

Nothing to it.

He rolled his shoulders. Stuck both his gloves in parka pockets and worked at slowing his breathing. How many times had he done this?

More than he wanted to remember.

He rested the barrel of the rifle on another branch, needing to compensate for the extra and unfamiliar weight of the suppressor. Then he zeroed the scope. Details sprang out in what had been a faraway scene. The length of a football field. Now, he could almost reach out and touch.

Slow and easy. Breathe in, breathe out. Wait for the natural rest.

Ten or fifteen minutes passed. Longer. Then suddenly a white-clad man appeared without Zach having heard him. Despite the warming day, he wore the hood up so that the fur almost obscured his face. He blended in remarkably well, only his boots gray or brown instead of white. The AK-47 stood out, of course.

Zach could have fired, but waited. *Closer, closer.*

Some instinct had his opponent sliding the rifle off his shoulder to ease it into firing position.

Can't let that happen.

Zach set the gun sights over the chest, safer than a head shot now that he knew the others hadn't worn Kevlar vests.

He let out a breath and gently pulled the trigger.

Dead on.

He'd have new nightmares, but refused to feel guilty. These bastards were hunting him and Ava relentlessly, as if planning to mount their heads on a wall.

He'd done what he had to do.

Chapter Twelve

With no way to tell the time, Ava could only guess. Each minute probably felt like fifteen. She strained her ears and eyes. It already felt like forever when she thought she heard… something. A *pop* that made her feel queasy. Then she decided she must have imagined it, because nothing else happened. Zach didn't appear, or call out to her to emerge from hiding.

She rested the gun on her thigh, holding it with her left hand every so often so she could flex the fingers on her right hand. How *could* it be so quiet? Why couldn't she even hear a bird call? It was as if nature held its breath. Maybe these old mountains and this forest resented the violence that invaded an ancient landscape meant to be a refuge. Except, these mountains also were home to several of nature's top-of-the-line predators.

What if she had heard a gunshot, only it was *Zach* who'd been shot? The thought sickened her, but after some deep breathing, Ava convinced herself she didn't believe that was possible, not for a minute. Zach had brought down *two* men when he was hurting and unarmed but for a folding knife. The next one, heavily armed, had come face-to-face with them, and Zach had outgunned him.

Who knew she'd ever be able to think so matter-of-factly about stuff that was so horrific.

No matter what, she kept her guard up. She flexed her fingers again, peered in every direction and strained for any sound at all.

IT HAD TO be an hour or more before the low call came to her. "Ava? Where are you?"

"Here." Her voice croaked. Her next effort was better. "Here!" She tried to stand but found her knees had pretty much locked. Still, she sent the closest cedar branches waving, and within a minute she saw him turning his head as he came into sight.

She staggered to her feet just in time. "Oh, thank God!"

He gave a weak grin. "Now, now. You need to have faith."

"I do," she said quietly, almost hoping he didn't hear her. From the way his gaze sharpened, she thought he had. "What happened?"

Carrying the rifle, he ducked into her shelter. "There was only one man on our trail. I went down almost as far as the river to be sure there wasn't a second one." He rested the rifle, butt down, against the tree trunk.

"He's dead?"

In the act of lowering his pack to the ground, he gave a clipped nod as he glanced quickly at her before looking away.

"Did you, well, learn anything?"

"No." With a groan, he sat down a couple of feet from her, leaning against the tree trunk. If she'd thought she had seen him tired before, it was nothing in comparison. He pulled off a glove and scrubbed his hand over his face and dug his fingers into his hair beneath the fleece hat. "Damn."

On instinct, she reached to lay a hand on the forearm he had braced on his knees. "I'm sorry. I wish I could do more."

The turbulence was back in his brown eyes. "Like kill people?"

The sharp edge in his voice shocked her. She snatched back her hand. "I should have said, I wish you didn't have to kill people."

"I'm the one who's sorry," Zach said heavily. "I hated doing it, but there wasn't any option except raising our hands and saying, 'Here we are, execute us.'" His mouth twisted. "*I'm* the executioner instead."

Feeling tentative, she said, "You said yourself that this is war. We *can't* let that monster loose on our country! Isn't this every bit as critical as whatever you had to do in, I don't know, Afghanistan or the other places you were sent?"

His eyes met hers. He didn't so much as blink for a minute before he finally dipped his head. "You're right. I know you are. I guess I've been getting mushy in my retirement."

She snorted, and one side of his mouth curled up.

"Okay. I'll quit with the self-doubt."

"Thank you. You saved both of our lives today. *Twice.*"

"Yeah, I guess so. Damn, I'm beat." His head turned again, as if he was evaluating her hidey-hole. "I'm thinking this is as good a place as any to spend the night. Maybe we can set up a little deeper in this stand of woods."

"Okay. Do you want to rest for a few minutes first?"

"Maybe." He tipped his head back and closed his eyes, thick dark lashes fanned on tanned, still discolored skin.

Ava let him brood, if that's what he was

doing. If he fell asleep…well, she'd find them a campsite and set up, then come back for him.

"This was another Russian," he said unexpectedly. "I'm betting ex-military. Probably all of them are. Were."

"That makes sense," she said softly.

"The odds are almost even now, except…" He broke off. "I wish I could keep you out of this."

"So far, you mostly have."

"If we could just get our hands on Borisyuk himself."

"Wouldn't it make sense for him to run for it?" She was practically begging for the answer she both wanted to hear and didn't, but also… There was no *logic* in a man whose goal was to disrupt this nation in some significant way wasting time to hunt down two snowshoers who, for all he knew, hadn't even had a good look at him.

Zach told her some of what he'd apparently been thinking about today, and she had to agree it was logical. And no, she didn't want Grigor Borisyuk to go on his way. Despite the struggles in her life, she'd never felt vengeful until now. She wanted that man to die next— or, better yet, for Zach to capture him and be able to hand him over to authorities.

THE END OF an operation was when you evaluated every decision, every pause, every command. Every hiccup. It wasn't Zach's habit to second-guess himself constantly mid-op, but he couldn't seem to help himself this time.

He did get himself moving so that he and Ava could find a secluded campsite even farther from the trail, but when she insisted on setting up the tent and rolling out the sleeping bags—and zipping them together again, his ears told him—he let her. He felt as if he'd been pounded.

He always had hated his rare sniper missions. He didn't know how the guys who did it day after day, month after month, came home even semisane. The combination of looking into someone's face so clearly, it was as if you could touch them, while they had no idea they were going to die, always sickened him. In modern warfare, it was necessary. He got that. But he'd rather any day be involved in a shootout across the street in some red-brown, dusty town, a straight-out battle where everyone involved knew what was at stake. Or having a hand-to-hand fight, as with the first two guys he'd brought down, even if he'd given himself the advantage from the beginning with the element of surprise.

Get it out of your mind, he told himself.

Which was fine, but then he devolved into thinking that, tired or not, he and Ava should have gone on, opened more distance between themselves and any pursuers.

Yeah, except it was likely one or two of these guys had also advanced up the ridge trail and would therefore be lying in wait for them. Better to face them after a good night's sleep. As good as he'd have, when he'd be keeping an ear out all night for any faint noise that didn't belong.

Ava broke into his brooding. "Any preferences for dinner?"

"Food."

She chuckled. "On our way out, maybe the helicopter would drop us in the parking lot at a pizza parlor."

"That sounds good to me." Now he was *really* hungry. He also liked that she pictured them together sharing a pizza. "I should have taken a turn cooking tonight. No reason for you to wait on me."

"An enlightened man," she teased. Then her voice and expression turned serious. "You're the soldier. I'm the one who has to wait. Of course I should contribute any way I can."

He frowned. "I'd be dead if it weren't for you, remember?"

"Yes, except if not for me, there probably wouldn't have *been* an avalanche."

"You're in a mood, aren't you?"

She closed her eyes for a moment, and her shoulders seemed to relax. When she opened her eyes, she fixed her gaze on his face. "I guess so. I *hate* waiting, not knowing what's happening to you. The last thing I should do is whine after you come back safe."

"Ava."

Her lashes fluttered a couple of times.

"You may be the bravest woman I've ever met. This has been a monumentally bad few days, and you've endured it all without any whining. You had to have passed the point of complete exhaustion and continued on for hours without a word at least a couple of those days." He smiled ruefully. "You cuddled with a complete stranger to warm him up. You popped his arm back into the socket. You let him leave you for *hours* in a hole that looked like an open grave. So let up on yourself."

Her mouth curved. "I will if you will."

He stiffened. "What are you talking about?"

"I know brooding when I see it."

Zach grimaced. "Set me up, did you?"

Wrinkled nose. "Kind of. I do feel useless, but I am smart enough to stay out of your way and help where I can. So let's eat, and go to bed the second it's dark enough to sleep."

He glanced around. "It's getting there fast."

"I know."

Dinner was a stew that he wolfed down, even though it wasn't very good. Ava had given him a much bigger portion than she ate. He saw that she'd opened three packets tonight instead of just two. Thanks to his scrounging, they had more than enough food.

See? There's a positive.

The candy bar was another positive, as was the cup of coffee. And knowing he'd be sleeping with Ava in his arms.

Tonight she boiled some water, and they took turns using a thin bar of soap, a washcloth and a towel. Each found privacy to scrub what they could. He imagined she was fantasizing about a hot shower as much as he was. He smelled his underarm dubiously before and after washing it, and couldn't decide whether there was any real improvement. Probably irrelevant, since he had no clean clothes. He hadn't felt he could afford the time, but he still regretted not ransacking the packs of the two men he'd shot in hopes one had been close enough to his size. But really, in the grand scheme of things, what difference did it make? On operations, he'd gone a lot longer than this without a shower.

None of this would have crossed his mind if it weren't for Ava.

He had reluctantly helped himself to a toothbrush from the first pack he searched, did his best to wash it clean of any germs and then used it. He wasn't going to subject Ava to his bad breath because he was squeamish about sharing spit with a Russian terrorist.

His outer layer of clothes went between the pad and the double sleeping bag. Lying down made him aware of every sore place in his body, yet was also such a relief that he groaned aloud. Ava, soon to join him, laughed, and he grinned at her. Her pencil flashlight lit up the interior of the tent enough to allow him to watch as she stripped off clothes, as well. Just not enough of them. As was their routine, he rolled, she spread them out with his, he rolled back onto the now double pad, and she turned off the flashlight before slithering in beside him.

Also as usual, she lay stiff for the first minute or two, until he reached out his right arm and pulled her into him. In no time, her head rested on his shoulder, her body pressed against his side and her hand lay splayed on his chest. He felt her fingers flex a little, and his body stirred. Making a move on her wasn't on the table, though, even if he thought she was attracted to him, too. He didn't like the idea she'd have sex with him because she was grateful, or how awkward it might be if she said hell no. A first for him, he might hate almost as much them making love only because she was thinking they could both die tomorrow and was grabbing for life with both hands.

Yeah, damn it, but what if they did die tomorrow, and had never—

He cut that train of thought right off. He wanted…something entirely new to him, and hadn't a clue whether she felt anything similar.

The remaining tension in her slowly eased. Eventually, she'd throw a leg over his. He also knew she wasn't asleep yet. Her breathing would change.

An owl hooted softly, not far away. He heard a squeak. Nothing to worry about, though. Letting himself relax toward sleep, he spoke without thinking.

"I feel as if I've held you like this every night for a lot longer than we've really known each other." He'd almost said, *For all my life.* Good catch, even if he shouldn't have said as much as he did. And, damn, suddenly he regretted every night he *hadn't* spent with her.

The ones to come, he couldn't let himself think about yet.

There was a minute tightening in her muscles before she whispered, "I…know what you mean. I've never been so comfortable before, or slept as well as I do with you, despite everything."

"I guess we fit together," he murmured.

"We do."

That sounded sad, which worried him, but he didn't know what he could do or say to make any of this better.

One more day, he told himself.

ZACH FELL ASLEEP before she did. Not that he snored, but…she could just tell. He was right. What would it be like in the imaginary future when she was able to go back to her life, crawling into a bed alone, shifting around, trying to find a place to rest her head that felt *right*? She'd never known before that she really needed, well, a body pillow to wrap herself around, too. Except, that body pillow wouldn't have a heartbeat; it wouldn't rise and fall in a gentle rhythm. It wouldn't be warm. And there'd be no strong arm around her, either.

She was grieving already.

I don't really know him, Ava tried to convince herself, but knew that was wrong. It was true they hadn't shared the trivial stuff people might on first dates: tastes in movies, music, books, favorite color, first celebrity or real crush. But none of that mattered. He'd told her things about himself that cut much deeper, giving her a glimpse of a complex man who probably suffered a degree of PTSD from his service. A man who, in an often-selfish world, was capable of enormous self-sacrifice. A man skilled at killing, who still showed kindness and an ability to understand what drove her, after knowing her less than a week.

She'd told him more about herself, and so quickly, than she had anyone else, too.

She was falling in love with him, Ava realized with less shock than she should feel. What to do about it…? Well, that wasn't obvious. Nor whether he felt anything similar for her. For heaven's sake, she hadn't even thought to ask whether he had someone waiting at home, a girlfriend or even a wife, although she believed he wouldn't have kissed her the way he did if that was so.

Worry about tomorrow, she lectured herself, and at last felt sleep claiming her.

Darkness was complete the next time she surfaced. Aware she'd half climbed on top of Zach, she puzzled over the big hand clasped over her butt cheek, while the other had found its way under her knit shirt to have a firm grip on her waist. First time that had happened. In her current state, she didn't mind. In fact, a hold so proprietary gave her a warm feeling of security. It let her slip back to sleep.

Some tension in the big body beneath her awoke her the next time. Was he holding his breath? Maybe he'd lifted his head slightly. She'd know, since she had tucked her face against his neck.

He was listening, she decided.

"Do you hear something?" she whispered.

After a long moment, he said, his voice low, "No. Probably came out of a dream."

He'd have plenty of nightmares to draw on, it occurred to her. As she herself did; frighteningly often, she reverted to being the hungry, desperate little girl who didn't dare trust anyone, who tried to be a ghost while stealing what food she could get her hands on and carrying it back to whatever nook she'd found that provided even minimal shelter.

She patted Zach's chest. A faint rumble rose beneath her hand.

"Comfortable?" he asked. And yes, that had to be a trace of amusement in the quiet question.

"Um…" She was suddenly unsure of herself. Okay, she'd been asleep, but she had taken an awful lot of liberties with his body. "Yes," she admitted.

"I like it." He squeezed her butt and rubbed his cheek against her head, catching hair on his short beard.

The position of her thigh, sprawled across him, had become a little less comfortable due to what felt like a bar on a sleeper sofa, but which she knew quite well was his erection. Arousal washed over her, tightening in her belly, melting down lower. Her nipples had to have hardened.

He'd notice.

Except…he was the one who'd started this.

"Ava?" he asked huskily.

She made a sound that might have been a whimper. When he wrapped both hands around her waist and lifted her, she went eagerly. Their mouths met clumsily in the dark. He had to pull back to swipe a long hank of her hair out of the way, but then they kissed with urgency like nothing she'd ever felt before. This contact was more important than anything in the world. His tongue thrust into her mouth, and she sucked on it, tangled her tongue around his, followed it back into the depths of his mouth. She tasted blood but didn't care.

She'd come to be straddling him, and even as they kissed, he gripped her hips and worked her up and down on his hard length.

"Swore I wouldn't—" he mumbled once, but she didn't let him finish. She didn't want to hear his qualms, or consider her own.

If she had any.

He found his way under her shirt to her

breast. Ava had never been more grateful that she had stripped off her bra every night for comfort. He cupped her completely, squeezed and rubbed gently, and oh, she wanted his mouth where his hand was, but even more she wanted—

"Let me," she said in a strangled whisper, and climbed off him enough to push her stretch pants and panties down. If only this was as simple as taking off a pair of jeans. Beside her, he had to be pushing his pants off, too, or did they zip or button open? Ava had no idea. At last, she contorted herself to grip the hem at her ankle and yank the wretched pants off that leg.

His fingers slipped between her thighs and her hips rocked.

"You feel so damn good," he said, in the voice like gravel. "I need you. Are you sure, Ava?"

"Yes." She'd given up getting the pants all the way off and flung her leg back over him.

"I don't have any—"

"I'm on birth control." A moment of sanity had her asking, "If you're—?"

"Yeah," he said hoarsely, even as he used his greater strength to position her, opening her.

As desperately ready as she was, he stretched her, filling her beyond capacity…except, after the first shock, she knew his size was just right.

We fit, he'd said, and they still did.

On her knees, she rode him even as he guided her, sometimes hurried her, slammed her up and down as she'd swear his entire body bowed up to meet her.

What hit her felt like the avalanche, a natural cataclysm, except being spun around and around was like flying, and she never wanted to come back to earth.

The pulsing inside her set her off again, something that had never happened before. She loved the raw sound he made that vibrated against her breasts as she collapsed against him.

In the sweaty, breathless, shaky aftermath, it would have been so easy to say, *I love you*. Instead, she made herself wait to hear what *he* would say.

It came after a minute, a ragged, "I never knew."

She'd never known, either. Scared as she was of making herself too vulnerable, Ava couldn't be a coward.

"Me, either," she whispered, closing her eyes to savor the way he stroked her, kneading occasionally, never stopping. *She* didn't move, because she didn't want him to slip out of her.

Turned out, she didn't have to worry, because faster than she would have thought possible, he was swelling inside her again, moving slowly, nudging her, until these impossible feelings rose in an inexorable tide, and they made love again.

Chapter Thirteen

Ava awakened to strong hands kneading her—butt, back, shoulders. It felt amazing.

"Morning," a gritty voice murmured in her ear.

She pried open her eyelids. "Not morning."

"Close enough. We want an early start."

She'd had such sensational dreams, and now came the hard clunk back to reality.

Not dreams. Oh, God. They'd made love *three* times, and each had been as good as the last. A quiver deep in her belly let her know that a fourth time would be absolutely fine with her, except… She let out a whimper. Or was it a whine?

"Sorry."

A last squeeze had her sighing before she squirmed her way out of the cozy, warm sleeping bag into frigid air.

He rolled the sleeping bags and pads with quick efficiency while she fired up the stove. Not fifteen minutes later, they were eating oatmeal with raisins in it and sipping coffee. Neither of them said a word about last night. She didn't know what to say, while he… Oh, he was a man. She'd been there, and why would they bother talking about it?

Ava suppressed a sigh.

Craggy and scruffy, his face came into focus as the sun rose. Ava was sure the lines beside his eyes hadn't been that deep the first time she'd climbed into a sleeping bag with him. His lips were even more cracked, as she could tell hers were. She grimaced, knowing she must look like something the cat had dragged in, as her last foster father had said. They'd both lost weight, despite the supplement to their diet. Think of the calories they were burning!

It didn't take her a minute to clean and repack the stove, pan and dishes, and not that much later she slid her booted feet into the bindings on her snowshoes.

"This is going to be rough," Zach warned.

She leveled a look at him that made him grin. Which lightened her heart, at least briefly.

He'd been right, she thought. Why bother getting into sticky emotions, assuming she wasn't the only one feeling them, when today might be the day they'd die?

The climb was a struggle. Occasionally, they had to remove their snowshoes to scramble up bare rock that tilted steeply upward. The rest of the time, they wound between stands of trees that became more stunted the higher they went. Obstacles lurked everywhere beneath the snow, some forming lumps, others dips: rocks, fallen trees, stumps, clumps of what might be huckleberry bushes or the like. Both kept having to untangle their snowshoes from whatever had seized them. Twice in the first hour, she went down and began to resent Zach's greater muscle mass that allowed him to stay upright even when he was tripped up.

He paused every twenty feet or so to scrutinize their surroundings. Ava appreciated the breather, but always felt her heart rate accelerate when his gaze paused on something or another and his eyes narrowed. She quit asking what he'd seen.

She was concentrating on where she put her feet when he said quietly, "There's the trail."

Lifting her head, she stepped on the back of one of his snowshoes and grabbed his parka for balance.

Crossing their current path, there were undeniable tracks on a level path covered in formerly smooth snow, but following those tracks with her eyes, she saw how the trail zigzagged to continue to climb steeply.

"Are they ahead of us?"

He leaned forward on his poles, studying what wasn't a clear-cut print. "Up and back, I think," he said at last. "This wasn't one man."

She absorbed that. "Do we dare—"

"Check your phone."

Ava lowered her pack to the ground, fumbled to open a pocket and removed her glove to touch the phone. She didn't have much hope, given that the trail had just started the steepest part of its climb, and if she turned in place she could see the surrounding Cascade peaks with dominating elevation. Still she stared at the phone in frustration. "Nothing."

"You've charged it?"

"You saw me!"

Ava stayed quiet and let him take out binoculars and scan, lowering them and frowning without saying anything. He was thinking.

Out of the corner of her left eye, she caught movement, or maybe the sun reflecting off something. Her adrenaline spiked.

"Zach?" she whispered. "Off to the left."

He whipped the binoculars in that direction just as she saw a flash of blue.

"Blue jay," she said in relief.

Zach studied the stunted trees growing amidst rock protruding from the snow for another minute. "Might have been scared into taking off."

She held her breath until, satisfied or temporarily dismissing any possible threat from that quarter, he turned the binoculars down the ridge again.

"Birds don't just hang out on branches all day, you know."

He didn't smile. She wished he would have.

"We have company coming," he said tightly. "Quite a ways down, but heading our way."

"They're afraid we went cross-country."

"That's my take."

"One, or the whole party?"

"I see only one man."

His eyes met hers. They were almost expressionless; this was the spec ops warrior looking at her. He'd quashed his emotions in favor of clinical decision-making and action. She would ache for the loss, but this part of him was the reason they were both alive.

"I need to stash you again," he said.

Somehow, she wasn't at all surprised by his pronouncement.

KEEP IN MIND *how fast two people heading toward each other will meet up*, Zach reminded himself as he strode as fast as the damn snowshoes allowed. *Set up an ambush, or gun him down.*

Zach didn't feel so much as a stir from his conscience this time. He no longer had the slightest doubt that this was life or death for him and Ava. Seeing the grenade launcher slung over this slug's back was the clincher. He had knowingly fired the shots to try to kill an innocent woman.

Never mind everything that had happened since.

Zach's mind seemed to have a split screen: his current surroundings and what he had to do, and Ava.

He didn't love the most recent hiding spot where he'd left her. The scattered clumps of stunted trees provided scant coverage because of the higher elevation. The best he could do was tuck her at the foot of a small drop-off along with both their packs. She couldn't be seen from the trail, but that didn't mean he felt comfortable with the choice.

She was armed, he reminded himself, but he lacked confidence she'd be able to pull a trigger to kill a man—at least, without hesitating too long.

Hell.

He'd done all he could. When he left, she'd had the handgun in a pocket of her parka where, worse came to worst, she could access it easily. At his last sight of her, Ava's bare hand had been buried in that pocket.

Concentrate on the war of attrition he was

conducting, he ordered himself. Four down, three to go. He couldn't afford a moment of carelessness.

His pace slowed. He'd rather set up, wait for the enemy to come to him. The idea of being too far from Ava ate at him. He hadn't liked the other times he'd left her, but this…

He traversed another switchback, finally spotting a small cluster of trees on top of a rock ledge that should allow him to see anyone coming up the trail before they saw him. Clothed in white, he should be hidden by the twisty group of mountain hemlock and subalpine fir.

He'd decided against setting any kind of snare. Lying in the snow, rifle set on a bipod, he might as well be in a shooting gallery. *Pop, pop*, done.

Zach used the binoculars sparingly under the theory that his target would be pausing regularly to use *his*. Best not to give him any warning.

He wasn't feeling real patient, though, and with every passing minute, his nerves stretched tighter. Could he have imagined seeing someone?

No.

Could the guy have halted before the pair of new tracks appeared on the trail and turned around to rejoin whatever compatriots he still had? Zach didn't believe that; any scout would have gone considerably farther before giving up. He wouldn't dare return too soon; Borisyuk would expect his minions to go to the last extreme.

Still, Zach detected no movement at all below him.

Disquiet had him feeling edgy and thinking hard. That peculiar, not-quite-itch crawled between his shoulder blades and up his neck.

What if the jay *had* been startled by humans? What if danger had been up the ridge, and the man Zach had seen was a decoy? What if that man had showed himself deliberately with no intention of advancing up the trail?

Without even knowing he'd made a decision, Zach was moving. Backing away from the edge, locking the bipod in place, hitching the rifle over his shoulder as he shoved his feet into the snowshoe bindings.

He was perilously close to panic. What if he was too late?

AVA WASN'T SURE she'd ever have the capability to wait patiently again, whether in line at the grocery store or to check in at the airport. This was torture, plain and simple. It had been all she could do not to beg Zach not to leave her. Only pride let her follow his instructions and do no more than whisper, "Stay safe," before he left.

Weird, when she thought about it, because her career was all about patience. She could lie for hours, impervious to stiff muscles or hunger, watching the entrance to a fox's den for a pup to emerge, or crawl into some absurd position in a tree where she could see the nest of a peregrine falcon. She'd been lucky enough that time to catch extraordinary photos of tiny beaks cracking open the shells, of the emergence of the babies and their first meal.

She'd like to think she could summon that kind of patience again, but right this second she wanted to scream.

He had a watch, but she didn't. Although, being able to see the seconds pass, wait for a minute to go by, then another, might make this worse. *A watched pot never boils*, right?

He'd asked her several times to have faith in him, and she did. Really. But he was one man against a terrorist sought by a good percentage of the governments in the world, and that terrorist had a squad backing him. Zach was still outnumbered three to one, and that was assuming their count from the photos she'd taken of the group on the ridge was accurate. There was no saying a couple more men hadn't been trailing well behind for some reason, or had gone ahead and already disappeared behind tree cover. What if there'd been a dozen more men?

For heaven's sake, she was talking herself into hysteria. Ava made herself take a few slow, deep breaths. So far, unless Zach had lied to her, he had hardly been challenged as he eliminated one opponent after another. There was no reason to think this would be any different.

Except she felt very, very alone.

A soft sound came to her. Her head turned sharply. Was Zach already back? Or—

A white-clad man reared above her on that rocky ledge. Her brain said, *Shoot him!* Her body tried to collect itself to move, but she was too slow. He sprang down, slamming her into the snow. Something cracked and pain shot through her. His gloved hand closed over her face, covering her mouth and nose. She couldn't breathe, couldn't scream. He'd broken her arm, Ava knew, which didn't prevent her fighting as viciously as she could to get out from under him.

She managed to get her mouth open and bit hard on what was probably mostly glove, but the man holding her down with sheer weight snarled something harsh.

He must have risen to his knees, because he wrenched her up, still stifling her ability to scream. She twisted and fought with everything in her. The next time she managed a bite, that big hand mashed so hard on her face she couldn't part her lips. Blood filled her mouth.

A calm voice behind her said something in that other language she assumed was Russian, and her captor turned her to face a second man who pointed a black handgun at her in a negligent way. If she hadn't already been terrified, the sight of him would have done it.

He was strange looking—not ugly, exactly, but as Zach had said, so distinctive no one would ever mistake that face. Cheekbones that, along with an exceptionally wide jaw, made the lower two-thirds of his face a square. As she stared at him, he pushed back his hood, and she saw the sharp widow's peak. The eyes that stared back at her were… No, cold didn't even describe them. Reptilian was closer to it.

Grigor Borisyuk himself. Ava knew this man would torture her to get what he wanted, and kill her with no more thought than most people gave to an ant on a sidewalk they'd accidentally stepped on.

It might almost be better if she was nothing to him but a problem he could solve with a snap of his finger. As it was, she and Zach had frustrated and inconvenienced him, and Ava suspected that wasn't a common experience for this monster in human form.

"You took pictures," he said, his English heavily accented. "I want your camera." He nodded at the other man, who loosened his grip on her mouth.

Could she talk without her teeth chattering? Her whole body wanted to tremble, but she made herself stiffen.

"My camera was damaged in the avalanche."

"You should have died." His eyes bored into hers.

"I was lucky." So lucky, she almost wished she *had* died, instead of being tormented by discovering hope and meeting a man she could—probably did—love.

"Give me the camera."

Scream? Ava knew she no longer dared. There was nothing to stop them from shooting her now and rooting through the packs on their own. She nodded as well as she could.

Another jerk of the head and the man holding her from behind spun her to face the packs. His rough handling must have grated the bones in her upper arm, because the pain that had been buried beneath shock and fear had her crying out.

She tried to reach out for the pack with both hands, but couldn't lift her left arm. She'd have to do everything with her right hand.

She'd still be able to shoot, she realized in a part of her brain that must be walled off from the emotional distress and pain. The man she'd fought, the one whose face she *hadn't* seen, must not have noticed the shape of what she had in her pocket.

She could dip her hand in that pocket right now.

No. She'd be dead before she could pull the gun out.

Wait.

With her right hand, she began fumbling with the zipper that opened her pack.

Was there any chance at all Zach would come in time?

SWEAT RAN DOWN Zach's face. It might be freezing, but he neither knew nor cared. Despite the steep climb, he was all-out running. His gut told him Ava was in trouble, that he'd been lured away from her. He'd felt a twinge of unease when that blue jay shot into the air. He'd have sworn if he could have spared the breath. He knew better than to ignore his own instincts.

At least one of the two remaining men had waited up above. Maybe both were there. If they'd seen where he rejoined the trail when he started down—they could go straight to Ava.

God. He needed to be more aware, not get himself shot because he was too single-minded, too afraid for her to care if he was the target instead.

He stopped, scanned. Continued, did the same. He didn't see any sign of life higher on the ridge.

That's because they weren't there anymore; he was terribly afraid they already had Ava.

Going up was slower than down, however hard he pushed himself. Sweat stung his eyes. He gasped for breath.

Soon, he had to get off the trail. Approach her position from an unexpected direction. Remember that he might still have one man coming up behind him.

Now, he decided, stepping gingerly onto a rock slab because he couldn't risk damaging his snowshoes. He took them off. Had to be quiet, too. Let Borisyuk and company think he was still down the ridge, fooled into thinking they had the upper hand.

AVA FUMBLED AS slowly as she could, which wasn't really pretense. The camera had settled down toward the bottom. First she pulled out the damaged lens, showing it, then dropping it on the snow when the Russian only sneered. She had to pull out packets of freeze-dried meals, rolled-up socks and wadded-up clothing, and let them fall, too. Finally she came to the camera and worked it out.

Borisyuk snatched it from her. The guy behind her tore off her hat and grabbed her braid, tugging her head back as if he enjoyed making her uncomfortable.

Of course he did.

Borisyuk brought the camera to life and began scrolling through photos. It took him time, but she knew the exact moment when he found his own face because he went completely still, not even blinking as he stared down at the screen.

His eyes scared her even more when he lifted them to her this time. "You have a… card. Or did you send this photo…?" He waved upward.

"I have a card."

"Do not play games with me. Show me."

Would he notice that there was a second slot for a different sized memory card?

Who was she kidding? Of course he would.

She indicated an empty slot.

"Where is it?"

"I—" Where had she put it? Her brain didn't seem to be working at top speed.

He backhanded her. Now her cheek hurt along with her neck. The man behind her laughed.

Borisyuk's cold gaze lifted, and he snapped out what sounded like a series of orders. The other man replied—argued?—and Borisyuk's face took on a cruel cast. He said a few more words that might have been ice pellets, but also raised the handgun to level it at her chest.

Her braid was suddenly released, and she bent her head forward in temporary relief as she sensed the second man rising to his feet. Finally, sidelong, she saw his back as he clambered back up the drop-off to where they'd presumably left their packs and snowshoes.

New fear squeezed Ava's chest painfully. He had been sent to watch for Zach—or even to join the hunt for him.

"Where is it?" Borisyuk asked again, and before she could open her mouth, the back of his hand connected with her cheekbone again.

Stunned, she had to blink a few times. If he knocked her out, he wouldn't get an answer…but maybe he didn't care. He could search her body and her belongings without any help from her. In fact, she wondered why he hadn't killed her yet.

"Where—"

"I have it," she interrupted, only her words didn't come out quite right. Her mouth must be swollen. She swallowed blood. She reached out again for her pack. She remembered slipping the card into a small, flat pocket near the top, probably designed for passports or driver's licenses or the like. It would have been easy to overlook, but refusing to produce the card would get her killed. Now, instead of later.

If he wasn't satisfied—no, she didn't *want* him to be, because then he'd be done with her.

She held it out, and he switched the gun to his other hand as he took the memory card from her. She dropped her own hand to her side and began inching it toward her pocket.

"There should be another one," he declared. "Give it to me."

Wham.

Her vision blurred. She wasn't sure she was seeing out of her right eye at all anymore. That meant *he* was right-handed, the way he was hitting her. Ava didn't know why that made any difference, but knew it did.

"My friend," she mumbled. "The man I'm traveling with. He has the other one."

She had never seen anything approaching the rage that built on Grigor Borisyuk's ugly face. His next blow knocked her over. She lay helpless on the snow as he glared down at her, the one memory card fisted in his hand, the gun pointing at her.

So much for her gamble. Why wouldn't he pull the trigger right now?

Chapter Fourteen

He heard voices and then a cry of pain, but also movement to his right. Zach threw himself flat onto the snowy ground, only slowly lifting his head. It was one of the men, but he passed out of sight before Zach could ready for a rifle or even pistol shot.

And did he dare do either? He gritted his teeth. Suppressors did just that, limiting the cracking sound everyone knew as gunfire. But they weren't true silencers by any means. Anyone with Ava was close enough to hear and recognize the peculiar *pop* if he fired now.

He wished he could be sure whether the guy had gone uphill or down. Or cut across the side hill to report back to Borisyuk, if that's who was with Ava.

Keep moving, he decided and rose. After taking a couple of steps that resulted in him sinking deep into the snow and leaving what looked like postholes, he awkwardly put the snowshoes back on. Soft as the snow was, he still sank, but at this point, tracks had ceased to matter.

Fear came close to clouding his ability to envision a scene and make a judgment. Ava cried out at nearly exact intervals, and each cry felt like a lightning bolt burning through his entire body.

Picturing the place where he'd left her, he realized he couldn't approach from below. Under the wide ledge, he'd be too low to effectively launch an attack, and too visible. Get back to the path he and she had used in the first place? That made him uneasy. There'd been a small bluff above her, which would have been the ideal way for someone to sneak up on her.

The cluster of trees didn't provide the kind of cover he'd like—they were too scrawny, too thin—but that still might be the best option.

Suddenly, two men were speaking what he thought was Russian. Ava was silent.

THE SECOND MAN came back twice to report to Borisyuk. Ava would have given almost anything to be able to understand what they were saying. Had he killed Zach and was now receiving congratulations? A growl in Borisyuk's voice suggested displeasure.

Where was Zach?

Through her daze of pain and with her blurred vision, she realized Borisyuk's attention was back on her. She was still on her knees, curled forward despite her best attempt at dignity.

"Why did you take my picture?" he asked.

"I—" She swallowed a mouthful of blood. "Whenever I'm looking at something, I click the shutter. I'm a wildlife photographer. That's why I'm here."

"You took—" he kicked her camera "—eight, nine pictures. Why?"

"Because…" She hesitated.

His hand blurred, coming at her so fast. Pain exploded.

She could only mumble.

"What? I cannot hear you."

"I was curious." She tried to form the words to his satisfaction. "Nobody should have been up on that ridge. I thought you must have crossed the border from Canada. There are no border checkpoints anywhere near."

The nearest she could come to describing his expression was displeasure.

"I saw the assault rifles some of the men carried. That…scared me. I thought I should report what I'd seen."

"Did you?"

Knuckles slammed into her face again, and she rocked in place.

Would he believe her if she lied? Would her answer, either way, make any difference?

No.

She swallowed more blood. Her tongue instinctively tried to find out whether he'd knocked out any teeth.

"No," she whispered. "Not yet."

"Your...*friend*?"

"I...don't know," she lied.

Wham.

This time she toppled sideways to the snow, landing on her broken arm. She'd thought it was almost numb, but now learned better. Had to keep her right arm free, though. Sooner or later, Borisyuk would get careless and she'd have her chance. Maybe the next time his teammate—no, his mercenary—returned.

"Do you know why I didn't kill you yet?" he asked in a tone of mild curiosity.

"No."

"You might be some use." He studied her. "You have a name?"

Nope, not me.

"Ava," she mumbled.

"Eva?"

"Ava. A-V-A."

He grunted, frowned and looked in the direction his man had disappeared.

She tensed, but before she could so much as stick her hand in her pocket to retrieve the gun, the Russian again turned that emotionless gaze on her.

She had to ask. "What use?"

"To, how do Americans say it? Ah. *Take care* of your friend."

Trap Zach. Persuade him to lay down his weapon with only the faintest hope they'd release her.

Don't do it, Zach, she pleaded. *They'll lie, then kill me, anyway.*

She was in enough pain right now, death didn't seem as frightening as it had.

Borisyuk bent and yanked her to her feet, his hand gripping her right upper arm with punishing force. "Stand." He pushed her a foot away from him. "You can stand," he said brusquely.

She could and did, but found it hard to keep her eyes open. Well, her left eye—she thought the right one was swollen shut. But she couldn't let herself sink into the dark abyss that beckoned, not while there was the slightest chance that Zach would save her—or that she could save herself. Or even him.

Borisyuk began to appear bored, if she

wasn't imagining things. *Yes, do think about your plans, your deadline, these irritating delays. Anything but me.*

He looked the same direction again. She squinted. No sign of that creep. Had Zach gotten to him?

But…was that movement, off to her left? The Russian hadn't noticed. She might be imagining that his boredom and indifference was shifting very slowly into tension.

She mustn't react at all. All she could do was wait.

Out of the corner of her only good eye, she could see a sliver of a man not quite hidden behind a wind-twisted tree. White arm, white hood framing his face, just as all those men wore. But it had to be Zach. What was he doing? Slowly, so slowly lifting a rifle into firing position.

Borisyuk was mostly behind her, so that she inadvertently blocked any shot. Would Zach risk it, anyway? That might be their only chance. Except, her captor thought she was helpless, and she wasn't.

If only Zach could draw his attention. The terrorist didn't seem to notice her hand creeping toward her right pocket. She couldn't pull the gun out unless he was distracted, but she could—her thumb found the tiny button that allowed her to turn off the safety.

With what felt like her last reserves, she ignored the useless left arm, all the pain, and poised on the balls of her feet to move faster than she'd ever moved in her life. She'd either shoot, or dive for the ground so Zach had no reason to hesitate. If Borisyuk heard anything and grabbed her, he could use her more effectively as a shield, and she couldn't let that happen.

She envisioned every action she had to take. Pull the gun out so smoothly it didn't get tangled with fabric. Or kick and dive.

"Grigor?" Zach called.

Borisyuk spun on instinct toward Zach. She yanked the gun out, leveled it, and just as the Russian thought to turn enough to grab her, she pulled the trigger, then pulled it again and again.

His gaze held hers as his own weapon fell from his hand, and then in eerie slow motion, he collapsed. It was like watching a puppet, animated one minute, losing all semblance of life when the strings were cut. He was dead before he hit the snowy ground. She could tell.

She backed up a step, then another, and finally dropped to her own knees to purge her stomach.

"Sweetheart." Zach was there, crouched beside her, hand on her back. "You're amazing. You'll be okay."

He kept his voice low, she thought in puzzlement. Didn't he know the monster really was dead?

And then she remembered there were still two more men, armed, alive and a threat.

SITTING ON HIS HAUNCHES, Zach wanted to haul her into his arms but knew he couldn't. Depending on her injuries, he'd hurt her, not give her comfort.

Deeper inside, he knew in horror how close he'd come to firing, despite the risk of hitting Ava. Thank God he hadn't. Thank God.

From the minute Ava looked up at him, rage joined the adrenaline-fueled emotions already so tangled he couldn't separate them. She looked bad, and would look worse once the bruises gained more color. Her right eye was too swollen to allow her to open it. She could have a broken cheekbone or jaw, or have had teeth knocked loose or out altogether. He'd seen pictures of women brutally damaged in horrific domestic violence episodes who looked better than she did.

Around the lump in his throat, he asked, "Where are you hurt?"

"My arm is broken." As swollen as her mouth was, the words were barely understandable. She touched her left upper arm in a tentative way that spoke for itself.

"I need to move you." He'd never hated saying anything more. "I assume that guy will come back—"

"Yah." Ava turned her head slowly, as if searching for her pack.

"No, for the moment, just you." He grabbed both handguns from where they'd fallen in the snow, switched on safeties and shoved them in pockets. He'd take Ava back the way he'd come, he decided. He had to pick up the rifle he'd dropped once Borisyuk went down, anyway, and he just needed to get her out of sight. "Can you stand?"

With his help, she rose shakily and showed no sign of collapsing. At his instruction, she put her right arm around his neck, and he scooped her up. Zach winced at the small cry that escaped her, but strode toward the tree cover, scanty as it was.

His thoughts scattered like a flock of pigeons at a clap of sound. He hoped there were still painkillers in that bottle she'd brought, or in one of the other packs. Borisyuk's and the other man's had to be nearby. What could he use for a splint? He could pack some snow on her face and the break—at least there was plenty of that. How quickly would the second man return—and what if the third one had joined him by now?

Zach wanted to get his and her packs out of there before reinforcements arrived. They wouldn't know how badly she'd been hurt, or how far away she could be. But he also needed—

"Is your camera working?" he asked.

She peered dazedly up at him. "Um...yah, if I can get...'nother lens on it."

"Photos with your phone would do," he realized.

A mumble answered him.

"Okay, I'm going to set you down here," he said, having seen a long crest in the snow that had to be a fallen log. Moving slowly to limit how much he jarred her arm or any other injuries, he bent and lowered her to a sitting position. "I need to grab our packs," he said. "I'll only be gone for a couple of minutes, but I want you to have protection."

That wasn't enthusiasm he saw on her face—truthfully, expressions on a face as battered as hers were next to impossible to read—but Ava accepted the handgun, flicked off the safety again and nodded at him. Her bare hand was probably freezing, but she didn't complain.

This was a woman who would never quit. The knowledge had his knees buckling with gladness that he'd met her, even as he wished she hadn't had to endure any of this.

Then he moved as fast as he could. He hurried to stuff her scattered possessions back into her pack before slinging it over one shoulder, his own over the other while carrying her poles and snowshoes. Now nothing remained in the vicinity except the body.

No—he frowned and scanned the trampled snow again. She'd have taken off the one glove to be able to shoot. But there was no sign of it.

He hustled back to where he'd left her, grateful to see her still upright and gripping the gun. He dropped everything in front of her and unzipped the pocket where he knew she stowed her phone.

She traded the gun for the phone and opened it for him, then they traded again.

As hard as he was listening, he wished he could swivel his ears like a rabbit, but no such luck.

Back to the clearing. As if he were a forensic photographer approaching a crime scene, he snapped pictures from a distance and then closer and closer before he rolled the body to get some clear ones of Grigor Borisyuk's dead face. Finally, he took a few more as he stepped back before dropping the phone in his pocket

He broke off a couple of low limbs from an evergreen and used them to try to mitigate his tracks from going and coming repeatedly. At best he blurred them, but had to hope that was good enough.

Once he was beside her again, he gently removed the gun from her hand and laid it atop his pack where he could easily reach it. The magazine had been full, and she'd only shot three or four times, he thought.

He dug in the jumble he'd made of her pack until he found some plastic bags, dumping out the contents—dirty clothes, he thought—and filling them with snow before wrapping each in some of those same dirty clothes. "Where's your glove?" he asked.

"Pocket." Or that was his best guess for what she'd said.

He found it, held it for her to insert her hand in. "I'm going to put this on the right side of your face. Can you hold it while I get a look at your arm?"

Ava nodded. Once he'd positioned the first ice pack against her face to cover her cheekbone, brow, eye and jaw, she raised her right arm and replaced his hand with hers.

Under almost any other circumstances, he'd

have cut off her parka to avoid hurting her, but he was painfully aware of how swamped she'd be in one borrowed from any of the men. None of them were small. Continuing to wear her own would be best. They still had to get to where they could make a cell phone call. If he had to leave her, the inactivity would make her especially vulnerable to cold.

So he carefully removed the glove on her left hand, said, "This is going to hurt," and started easing the arm of the parka off. She couldn't entirely stifle a few whimpers and cries, and he apologized nonstop, grimacing the entire while.

He couldn't put either of them through this again. The fleece quarter-zip and turtleneck she wore beneath were replaceable, so he used the wicked knife he'd taken from one of the packs he'd rifled and cut the fabric at her shoulder. If only he had scissors—

Since he didn't, he sliced the sleeves from the top down to her wrist until they fell off.

It wasn't hard to see the break.

Still holding the ice pack to her face, Ava craned her neck to peer down at her upper arm. "I hab…" She licked some blood from her lips. "First aid kit."

The reminder was good. He hoped she hadn't used up most of what the kit held treating him. Once he dug it out, he marveled again at how prepared she'd been when setting out on her trek, knowing she'd be beyond help if she injured herself. He found a foam splint, and, though it wouldn't match a cast, it would help until they reached a hospital.

First, though, he pressed the other bag full of snow against the grotesque swelling.

Her slit of an eye fixed on him. "Otter mun?"

O... Other. Other man.

Zach shook his head. "I set up not far down the trail and waited for him, but when he didn't appear I got worried that he was a decoy."

"Was."

"Yeah. I hauled ass back to you, but I heard voices before I reached you."

She bobbed her head. "Knew you'd come."

He had to be getting better at understanding her thickened mumbles. He wished he could put an ice pack in her mouth, which was bloody. Had she bitten her tongue? Lost teeth? God. "I almost didn't." He was tortured with the knowledge of how close he'd come to being too late. The vicious ache felt as if a blow had cracked his sternum.

"Did."

Zach closed his eyes and bent to press his lips very softly to the cheek on the—mostly—uninjured side of her face.

Her worries now almost had to echo his.

"I could go out to the trail and shoot anyone who shows up, but that would mean leaving you alone." Vulnerable. "Not doing that again."

A tear had leaked from one corner of her eye.

"I wish I knew what they'll do when they find Borisyuk dead." Go for revenge? Or run for their lives? The answer depended, again, on whether they were hired muscle or dedicated zealots.

And where was the guy who'd left just as Zach arrived? Lying in wait along the trail, thinking he could pick Zach off? Meeting up with his buddy?

Zach wished he could be a hundred percent sure there *were* only two men remaining. He hadn't said anything to Ava, but he knew the group they'd seen up on the ridge could have been strung out far enough that they hadn't all been visible silhouetted against the sky. If so, they might be spread out watching other trails, per orders.

A faint, alien whisper of sound reached him, and he stiffened. Obviously watching him, Ava did the same. She set down the snow pack and picked up the handgun.

Zach cocked his head, waiting.

It came again, not quite a *swish-swish*,

but walking in deeper snow was a lot harde
work than striding along a trail. One man
he thought. He rose to his feet, careful not t
make a sound, and lifted the rifle from where
he'd propped it against his pack.

That someone moved past them, higher up
the ridge than where they'd holed up. Anglin
in to rejoin Borisyuk? Damn, Zach wished h
and Ava had been able to move farther away
If this guy chose to use his fully automati
rifle to spray bullets in a circle, he could mov
them down.

Zach held out a flattened hand to indicate
that she should lie down. Without a word o
so much as a cry of pain, she slid to her knees
then half rolled over the log where she'd bee
sitting so she would be behind it.

He eased behind the largest tree in this smal
clump, even knowing it was inadequate cover
Better than nothing.

Then he fitted the butt of the rifle to hi
shoulder, rested the barrel on a branch and fo
cused through the scope. Through it, he clearl
saw the one guy, who had seemingly left hi
snowshoes up above but jumped down an
rushed to Borisyuk. The very clarity offere
temptation. Had this man been guilty of injur
ing Ava? Zach's finger tightened slightly on th
trigger, but he waited. Despite everything, h

found himself thinking again like a cop instead of the soldier he'd been. That didn't mean, if this bastard made one wrong move—

But he didn't. Shock appearing, he made a hoarse exclamation, looked around in panic and then turned to scramble back up the steep rise. He made a lot more noise retreating than he had arriving.

Zach swung around and moved quietly in turn toward the trail, feeling Ava watching as he passed her.

A pack slung over his back now, the visitor was hustling down the ridge. Running. For help, or with the intention of fleeing?

Lowering the rifle, Zach wished on one level he'd killed the SOB, diminishing the count by one. Fine time to be hit again by how much he disliked killing, seeing death on those men's faces.

After a minute, he returned to Ava, who in turn lowered the handgun down. "I think we have time," he said. "Let me help you up."

Time, at least, to splint her arm to the best of his basic medic ability, get some painkillers and something to eat in her, and figure out whether she was capable of striking out for the ridgetop.

Chapter Fifteen

Zach had kept wincing as Ava tried to eat the snacks he poured into her hand. The raisins weren't too bad, but her jaw hurt too much when she tried crunching on almonds or even peanuts. Eventually, he'd conceded that she had done the best she could, and the super dose of ibuprofen he'd convinced her to swallow didn't seem to be upsetting her stomach. Not that she was sure she'd notice, given how much she hurt. No, not true—she distinctly remembered puking after she'd shot and killed a man, so close up she'd never be able to block what she'd seen from her memory.

Her arm felt marginally better after Zach set it—he claimed it was a clean break—splinted it and then constructed a sling from a turtleneck shirt he ripped and reshaped.

"It's getting later than I'd like," he said finally. "I'd hoped we could make it up high enough for cell service today, but I don't see how that can happen. We can't stay here, either, though, not without knowing whether the two remaining men will come gunning for us."

"Why would they?" she tried to say.

Seemingly understanding her, he shrugged. "Because they're enraged? I don't know what they'll do, and I don't like that. We can't forget they're out there."

She was in no danger of forgetting.

"I think we should combine whatever we think we really need into one pack now. My suggestion is that we go up the trail and watch for someplace we can camp for the night that isn't quite so close to, er…"

The body. The man she'd shot dead.

The farther the better, in her opinion. She felt weird, but also steadier than she had. Yes, she hurt, but Zach must have hurt as much after the dislocated joint and head injury, and he'd been able to cover miles. *His* head had been slammed by a wall of snow and blocks of ice. Borisyuk had wanted to hurt and scare her, but she doubted the force he'd applied had been remotely comparable. If Zach could go on after that, so could she.

"Head?" she asked, tapping his temple with a gloved finger.

His alarm was obvious. "Your head worse?"

"No. *Your* head."

He gave a bark of laughter. "You're worrying about *me* after you've been beaten to a pulp? Today's been eventful enough, I've kind of forgotten about my headache. I think it's mostly gone, though. No more dizziness or double vision."

She scowled at him, then wished she hadn't. "Didn't tell me—"

"I didn't want to worry you."

Ava would have rolled her eyes if she could have. Any woman would have had the sense to tell her partner that she was having worrisome symptoms so she'd have someone to watch out for her. Superman here hadn't wanted to worry her.

He'd also saved her life several times over, she reminded herself.

"Can go on," she managed to say.

After a sharp look at her, he turned his attention to inspecting the contents of both packs, discarding a good-sized pile, then repacking with an occasional addition or subtraction made by her. She was secretly glad he hadn't fetched Borisyuk's pack. She didn't want anything out of it.

As if their minds were in tandem, though, Zach sighed. "I need to find Borisyuk's pack. See if there's anything I should take from it."

"Don't want—" she protested, but he shook his head.

"He might have carried something that will tell us who his target was, the contact info for whomever he was meeting up with, that kind of thing. In case the pack isn't here anymore when the border patrol comes for the body."

"Oh." That made sense.

He left her with his usual precautions, and she listened hard until he returned fifteen or twenty minutes later, moving so quietly she didn't hear him until he was close enough to startle her. His grim expression didn't surprise her, but she didn't ask what if anything he'd found. There'd be time for that; she had to believe that, after all this, they'd make it.

He attached one of her poles to the pack before helping her into her snowshoes and to her feet. Eyes keen on her face, he was obviously watching for any hint she was about to collapse. Even though she didn't want to take a step, Ava was careful to hide how awful she really felt.

So, okay, she did understand why he'd done the same thing when they'd absolutely had to keep moving those first couple of days.

Progress was painfully slow as they slogged toward the trail, sinking into deep snow, tripping over the usual hidden obstructions. Seeing how desperately he wished he didn't have to put her through this kept Ava strong. The one time he had to pick her up and she tried to give him a reassuring smile, though, she saw immediately that the attempted smile had had the opposite effect. Not one of her best, apparently.

Once they neared the ridge trail, he left her again to reconnoiter. Returning, he said tersely, "Don't see anyone."

She nodded and followed him.

I can do this, she told herself fiercely, and kept repeating it.

The way was easier on the actual trail, especially because of the other tracks going both up and back on it. At least it had been maintained well enough through the autumn; it was mostly free of fallen limbs and rocks. What's more, at this elevation, they were leaving behind the tree line. She could tell Zach didn't like being so exposed, but he'd have been on edge no matter what their surroundings. The enemy was still out there, and he had to protect her.

She quit keeping tabs on him and bent all her concentration on the next step. Every movement hurt her arm and head. Even reverting to thinking, *Left foot, right, left*, was beyond her.

She plodded and focused on the tracks right in front of her, blocking out everything else.

She could and was doing this.

ZACH HAD SEEN teammates injured and going on with that same intense focus, but watching Ava moved him beyond anything he'd felt before. A couple of hours ago, she'd had her arm snapped and then been beaten; she could only use one pole, and he knew damn well the dose of ibuprofen he'd given her hadn't done more than slightly mute the pain. Yet there she was, marching on up the switchbacks of a precipitous climb.

If he asked her, he knew she'd say she could keep going as long as necessary, but unlike her, he'd been keeping an eye on the sinking sun. He was desperate to reach the top, prayed the phone could make contact from there to a cell tower, but no matter what, they didn't dare continue once the light started to fail.

What worried him was that she'd feel worse in the morning than she did now.

He bared his teeth in a grimace that she, thank God, couldn't see. No, that was one of a long list of worries. At the top was staying aware that Borisyuk's two or more remaining men could be hunting them. He stopped frequently to use binoculars to scan behind them.

Unfortunately, not even high-quality binoculars could penetrate the dense woods low in the valley. All he could do was be sure no one could sneak up behind them.

Remembering the grenade launcher kept that irritating prickle crawling along his spine. They were out of range now, he was confident—unless someone else awaited them at the top of the ridge.

At last he spotted what he'd been looking for—a small cluster of subalpine hemlocks, able to survive where other trees couldn't because of their slender profile and down-sweeping branches that shed heavy snow. Below them was a sharp drop-off, so no one could approach from that direction. He hoped there was a level spot that would allow two people to stretch out, but even if they had to sit huddled against each other, this was the best they were going to find.

"Ava. Wait."

She stopped but didn't even look back. Just stood there, confirming his belief she was at the end of her rope.

He came up next to her and pointed with his pole. "We'll spend the night there."

Still without looking, she nodded.

"Wait until I make sure it's accessible." Without pausing for a response, he left the trail, every movement cautious. He quickly discovered he was clambering along a rocky ledge. A fall wouldn't be great, and likely would ensure broken bones or heads. With each step, he stamped his foot a couple of times to bare the rock as much as he could. There'd be no hiding the trail he and Ava would make—but he already knew he didn't dare sleep tonight.

As he'd hoped, the trees had been able to take root because of a deposit of soil, however thin and rocky, left in a small dip on the mountainside. Zach poked around and found a clear place large enough to set up the tent, although he didn't plan to do that. He wanted a 360 degree view around them.

He set the pack down and went back for Ava. A dull gaze lifted to him when he appeared in front of her.

He'd rather carry her, but when he offered, she said, "I can keep going." Of course she did.

"Okay. Follow my tracks. The rock isn't far beneath the snow. I'll be right behind you."

With that same absolute concentration, she trod in the path he'd laid, one cautious step after another. Behind her, he stayed poised to lunge forward and catch her if he had to—but she reached his pack and stopped.

He laid out pads before he gently helped her step out of her snowshoes and sit down. Even with his arm around her, lowering herself to the ground clearly hurt like hell. Zach discovered how much he hated seeing her suffering, but all he could do was try to make her as comfortable as possible.

He wrapped the sleeping bag around her shoulders, then encouraged her to sip water. Without complaint, she held another snow pack to her face while he got out their stove, fired it up and peered into a couple of packets of freeze-dried meals before finding what he wanted—one that would probably taste more or less like the stew it purported to be, but didn't appear to have much texture.

In fact, heated, it looked a lot like canned dog food, but didn't smell bad.

To his dismay, Ava looked vaguely surprised when he held the pan in front of her. Had she not noticed that he was cooking? How bad was her concussion?

But then she mumbled what he thought was "Thank you" and took the spoon from him. He stayed close to wipe her face when she didn't quite get every spoonful in her swollen mouth, and to take over after her hand started to shake.

Most of it went down, though, and when he took the pan away she met his eyes.

"D'ank you."

She was all there. Thank God. He smiled.

"You're welcome. This isn't as good as the meals you brought, but…"

She lifted fingertips to her lips.

"Easier to eat," he finished, and she nodded.

Zach wolfed down his own portion, wishing it was a greasy burger with cheese and an extra-large serving of French fries, although pizza would have been fine, too, or real stew with tender chunks of meat and potatoes.

He'd have liked to think, *Soon*, and believe it, but couldn't quite. There was no guarantee they'd find cell phone service even at the top of the ridge. As for their next step… He hit a wall. Yeah, he was tired, but he would figure it out when he had to.

After cleaning up, he readjusted the sleeping bag so he was under it with Ava, and settled for cuddling her. She lay her head on his shoulder and just…rested. The unfamiliar warmth in his chest felt like happiness, despite their perilous circumstances.

It had to be fifteen minutes before she mumbled, "Missed pickup."

"Yeah." He'd had other preoccupations, but now that she'd reminded him… "I never heard a helicopter."

She shook her head, he assumed to say that she hadn't, either.

"When you didn't show, they should have mounted a search."

"Maybe just think I'm late?"

"Alone out here? They're irresponsible if they don't ask the park service to start looking for you." That would have cheered him more if he'd heard any helicopter however far away, but still, at the top of the ridge, he and Ava would be highly visible. Too bad there'd be no wood, dry or otherwise, to build a fire that would draw attention.

Against his upper arm, she tried to say something. He had to pull back and raise his brows.

"Wish we had…"

She was back to dwelling on that damn satellite radio. He shook his head. "None of that. We've made it this far. We'll make it the rest of the way."

Given her swollen face, he couldn't be positive, but he thought Ava was peering deep into him, seeing… Who knew? His confidence?

Or was it pretense she saw?

He said, "Why don't you lie down? You can use me as a pillow."

Not easy to arrange, but it worked.

BECAUSE OF THEIR increased elevation, darkness came a tiny bit later. Between mountains, Ava even saw a lingering, gradual deepening of the sky rather than the sudden plunge into night to which she'd become accustomed.

She held on until twilight made it hard to see at all, and despite the pain that tried to consume her, she fell asleep. Or lost consciousness. Rousing several times to darkness, shifting in futile attempts to find a more comfortable position, she knew Zach never slept. Each time, his hands were there, reassuring, helping her settle, his touch tender, his voice husky and words comforting. She couldn't have said whether she'd been in a coma or truly asleep. If there were dreams, they didn't linger.

This time when she opened her eyes, the sky had lightened enough she could see Zach's face above her. She lay on her side, she realized, arm propped on the pack, head on his thigh. He seemed to be staring contemplatively down at the intersecting valleys now far below them, until he must have become aware she was awake—she'd tensed, or her breathing had changed. Who knew?

"Hey, sunshine." He smiled, peeled off a glove and cupped the less painful side of her face with a big, warm hand.

She nestled into it.

"Don't suppose you're feeling your best," he murmured.

Ava thought about it. "Yesterday, I didn't think I'd live to see this morning," she pointed out. And, wow, her speech sounded clearer, didn't it? Had her swelling gone down?

His dark eyes never wavered. "Think you can sit up?"

Think about, maybe. Actually doing it…not so much. But…she had to, didn't she?

"Yes?"

He laughed at her. "Heartfelt positivity."

She'd have wrinkled her nose, but had a bad feeling it was broken. Maybe her cheekbone, too. Teeth… She ran her tongue over them. Thank goodness, they were all there, although a couple felt like they might be loose.

Just as well she hadn't brought a mirror.

He helped her as she raised herself an inch at a time, groaning. Zach supported her lower arm with one hand until she was upright, then tied her makeshift sling back into place. The water in the bottle was almost too cold to drink, but she washed several ibuprofen down with it, anyway, then waited eagerly for the pills to take effect.

If they did, the effect wasn't all that noticeable, but she was able to eat the oatmeal he prepared, and savored every drop of her cup of tea, even if he'd overloaded it with sugar.

Drinking his own, he scratched his jaw irritably.

"Itch?"

"Like crazy."

She'd almost forgotten what he looked like without the scruff that had now become a shaggy beard. At least it helped keep his face warm.

At last, reluctantly, she asked, "What's the plan?"

Regret in his eyes, he said, "I think we need to find out whether you *can* go on. I hate the idea of leaving you, armed or not. These guys can shoot from such a distance, you might not even know they're coming."

She shivered.

"Damn." He leaned forward. "I'm sorry. I shouldn't have said that."

"No. Should. Need a motivational talk."

He glowered at her. "Are you making fun of me?"

"Maybe?"

Zach grunted, but one corner of his mouth lifted.

"Not that far."

"No. Maybe a couple of hours should see us at the top. We'll have wide visibility there, which'll give us an advantage if anyone is behind us. Otherwise…"

She patted the pocket of her pack holding her phone.

"Yeah." He cleared his throat. "Might be worth a prayer or two."

THE WORST PART was getting started. Every joint creaked, every muscle hurt as if she'd wrenched it. Her head felt as if it had blown up to twice its size and her neck wasn't adequate to keep it upright. It throbbed. Her dark glasses didn't seem to block the glare; she kept wanting to close her eyes—okay, eye—but fought not to succumb. For Zach's sake.

But gradually, as she warmed up, she found she was moving more easily, the lift and stride in the snowshoes natural. She'd have given a lot to be able to use both poles, but considering the alternative—say, getting shot, her body abandoned like trash in the snow—this wasn't so bad.

To Zach, her pace undoubtedly felt like slow motion, but he never forgot about her long enough to let any significant space open between them. She knew he was pausing frequently to watch her, but she didn't let herself meet his eyes. Better to empty her mind as much as possible and just keep going.

He did insist they stop once, making her eat a handful of raisins and drink some water, but kept it brief. He must've been afraid her body would stiffen.

More than it already had.

For a while, she counted legs in the switchback, but really that didn't help, since she had no idea how many remained ahead of them. Her concentration waned. She kept moving, but wasn't thinking at all. Just step, swing pole, step. Once warmed up, her legs didn't feel bad, but her head and arm coalesced into blazing agony. The last coherent thought she had was, *How had Zach done this?* And for days?

"Sweetheart."

She liked him calling her that, but didn't let herself break stride. If she stopped now, Ava wasn't sure she could start again.

She collided with him, teetered, and let him catch her in his arms.

"We're here. You made it, Ava."

Here? After blinking a couple of times, she turned her head and saw that the trail had leveled off, and a dazzling panorama surrounded them. Even so, with her mind working sluggishly, it took her several minutes to understand. They'd reached their goal. He was right: she *had* made it. Only...

He said it for her. "Now's the moment of truth."

Chapter Sixteen

Ava's phone produced a single, flickering bar, and that was after Zach tromped knee-deep in snow in circles for a good ten minutes, pointing the damn thing every which direction. When he saw that small flicker, he froze.

"Got it." And if he so much as twitched, he'd lose it.

"Oh, thank God." Ava didn't try to get up from where she sat with the pack.

Trying to hold the phone completely steady, he tapped in his friend's phone number. Then he held his breath…to no avail. The call could not be completed.

Unsurprised, he thought some foul words.

"Text," Ava said from behind him.

Yeah, they sometimes went through when a call wouldn't. Naturally, he lost the bar while he wrote a short message saying, basically, Borisyuk dead, need pickup for two, the ridge identified. It took Zach two or three minutes to find the perfect spot again to recover that fragile, single bar. He pressed the arrow to send the text on its way, and held his breath again. He didn't so much as blink while he stared at the phone.

Was there any way to know if a message reached its goal? He had no idea. What if it had gone through fine but Reid was busy, didn't check his phone for five minutes or five hours? Zach wouldn't get any response unless he stayed as still as a statue—or found this exact spot again. Damn, he should start thinking about plan B—

A message popped up with startling speed.

What the???? Your ride on the way as fast as I can find a pilot and get the chopper in the air.

Blown away, Zach tried to take it in. He could only imagine the confusion, consternation, hope that his few words would have aroused on the other end.

He sent back a thumbs-up, pocketed the phone and turned to Ava.

"They're coming," he said simply.

Her mouth trembled and a couple of tears leaked from her open eye. She hadn't believed this would work.

He felt like whooping, picking her up and

swinging her around, kissing her until they both forgot where they were…but of course he couldn't do any of that. Who knew how far an exuberant yell would carry in the vast quiet?

So all he did was sit next to her, gently kiss her cold cheek and dig in the pack for something to eat and for the water bottle.

He couldn't find any raisins. The dried apricots and other fruits would take some serious chewing. He offered her peanuts again, and she stared at them with an expression of loathing before taking the small packet from him.

"French fries. *Salty* French fries."

He laughed, joy welling up from deep within him. "Hate to tell you this, but you'd be sorry if you ate anything salty with your mouth in that condition."

Her sound of frustration made him laugh again. For a few minutes, he let himself savor being able to sit beside her, his arm around her back, her head tipped against his upper arm. Along with a tangle of other emotions, he felt an unfamiliar sense of peace.

Of course, it couldn't last, since he wasn't foolish enough to forget their potential pursuers. He and Ava would have quite a wait…and they were more exposed up here than he liked.

He downed a good-sized handful of raw almonds, swallowed some water and made himself get back to his feet. The binoculars still hung around his neck, and the rifle leaned against the pack, ready for him to grab.

"DAMN." ZACH'S FRIEND Reid had to shout to be heard in the noisy helicopter. "That's really him." He hadn't torn his gaze from the screen of her phone. He sounded incredulous, for which Ava didn't blame him. Really, what were the odds that a noted terrorist had crossed the border here, in Washington State, and that in this vast wilderness, his retired army friend out for some winter camping had happened to stumble upon him?

Ava watched from her seat, *not* designed for comfort, and tried to keep her teeth from chattering from the vibration. She didn't mind flying—although she definitely preferred a big jet to a small plane—but really didn't enjoy helicopters. She'd had no choice but to take one to drop her in the midst of the park. This time, though... Well, it had appeared like an angel from on high. She hadn't fully believed she and Zach had survived until she saw that helicopter swooping toward them. She was afraid she'd actually cried at that moment, although she'd wiped away any tears before the copter gently settled onto the snowy top of the ridge.

Zach had wanted her to be conveyed straight

to a hospital, while Reid argued for them to first retrieve the terrorist's body and pack. Ava had shaken her head to silence Zach's protests. The border patrol agents and maybe somebody like the National Guard would undoubtedly swarm through this segment of the park once they heard the whole story, but that would take time to organize, and she understood their priority. She wasn't dying. What difference would another hour or two make?

Only to herself did she admit that the detour also gave her a little longer to watch Zach and to revel in his frequent, searching glances. He hadn't put her out of his mind the second that rescue had arrived. Once this helicopter did land on a hospital helipad, she knew she'd be whisked away while he involved himself in the hunt for the remaining terrorists and the maybe rescue of the one he'd left trussed up, to use his words.

Ava had no doubt she'd see him again. They'd become close enough that she believed he would come to see her, verify that she had arrangements in place to go home, and to say goodbye.

It was the goodbye part that she dreaded.

She'd lost track of how many days and nights they'd spent together since she had started across the avalanche slope with the uneasy awareness that a man was behind her, maybe even chasing her, and gaining ground by the minute. It had to be less than a week…but one of heightened emotions, physical exertion like she'd never imagined and a reliance that went both ways with an extraordinary man. The before felt…pallid, in comparison. Or maybe not even real. Her future was a blank.

It was silly to mourn the loss of a man she knew in one way, and not at all in others. There'd never been any chance that— what?—he'd throw over his life to follow her to Colorado? That he'd want to have her waiting patiently for him at home every day, once he could get away from his real life investigating crimes? That didn't sound like him, or her.

But for the first time in her life, she knew she'd make sacrifices to be able to stay with him.

Ava pushed at even that acknowledgment. The intensity of what they'd shared would fade. What felt most real now no longer would as the days passed, as she downloaded her photos and became absorbed in editing, settled into her usual routine.

She turned her head to see him watching her again, lines furrowing his forehead, concern in his dark eyes. She tried for a weak smile that failed to smooth those deep lines at all or lessen the intensity in his expression.

Habit, she tried to tell herself. The bond they'd formed would take time to thin and eventually disappear. Given his many deployments and the losses in combat, this experience was probably familiar to him. One minute, the people around you meant everything, the next, you said your goodbyes and flew back to a base where you had to reconnect with friends and family you'd left there.

Ugh. Knock it off.

Things became tense—snapped orders, cold washing in the open door of the helicopter as it hovered above the snow-covered ledge where she and Zach had left the body of the man she'd shot and killed.

Something else not to think about.

Apparently the body was still there. The pack, too, she saw, when Zach was winched up carrying it on his back. The body... Ava looked away at that point. The two men deposited it somewhere behind her.

Then, as the helicopter rose into the air again, Zach came to sit beside her.

"Hadn't been touched," he shouted. "The two survivors must be on the run."

"What about...?"

His eyebrows climbed. "The guy I left alive?"

She nodded.

"He's our next stop, if I can pinpoint the place from the air. Although—" now he sounded bleak "—I doubt he could hold out this long."

Of course he hadn't forgotten the one man he'd been able to leave alive. She reached over and squeezed his hand, rewarded by the way their eyes met and held.

She did know him. She did.

TO ZACH'S ASTONISHMENT, Jarek Krasnitskiy— or so his passport claimed him to be—was alive. In bad shape, but bundled for warmth, given oxygen and fluids, he would soon be in the hospital along with Ava.

Zach had known he wouldn't be able to stay with Ava until everything he knew, had done and had thought since he first saw those men silhouetted atop the ridge had been sucked out of him. He had no doubt agents would pounce on her, too, once doctors gave them the go-ahead.

After watching her get placed on a gurney and rushed into the hospital, he went to the local border patrol headquarters and submitted to the interrogation. He did his best to put

Xs on the detailed topographic map, showing where he and Ava had first spotted the men—and where the other bodies could be found. Somebody, somewhere, would have to decide whether he was justified in shooting and killing, but his conscience felt clear. He and Ava wouldn't be alive if he hadn't had the skills he'd brought home from his service in dangerous parts of the world.

When they were done with him, at least temporarily, he called a taxi to take him to the hospital. A receptionist directed him to Ava's room. The door marked with the right number stood half-open. As he pushed it fully open and started into the room, a nurse hurried toward him.

"I'm sorry. Visitors aren't—"

"We're friends," he said. "I was with her when she was hurt."

Her lips compressed, but she nodded. "Please keep your visit short. Authorities are eager to talk to her, but Dr. Chavez has refused them access."

Zach smiled at her. "Good."

His first sight of Ava in the hospital bed took him aback. Her face looked even more discolored and swollen against the white pillowcase. Her eyes were closed and her body appeared slight beneath the sheet and thin blanket. He couldn't see the vibrant woman who had dug him out of the grave made from snow, ice and rock, who had warmed him with her own body…until her eyes suddenly opened.

One was still a slit, but the deep blue color was apparent. "Zach. Is everything all right?"

Despite appearances, the swelling was definitely decreasing, giving her speech improved clarity.

"Yeah." He cleared his throat. "Let me find a chair."

He pulled one from under the window to her bedside, then sat down and reached out without thought for her hand that lay on top of the covers. Their fingers twined together, the action so fluid they might have held hands through years instead of days.

"I see you got a cast."

"Yes, and it helps." Her nose crinkled. "Whatever they're pumping into me through the IV helps even more, I suspect."

He grinned. "I have no doubt. You had to be dehydrated besides. I'll bet you've lost a lot of weight."

Her gaze seemed to drink in his face. "You, too. You've had something to eat?"

He cleared his throat. "Ah…"

"A cheeseburger. And fries?"

Had she caught a whiff of his breath? "Afraid so."

Ava made a sound that expressed indignation.

"Maybe I can sneak something in. I assume they're keeping you tonight?"

"Yes. They think I had a concussion."

No kidding.

She frowned. "You should get looked at, too."

"I'm feeling fine." Exhausted, relieved, grateful and scared about how she'd respond when he talked to her about the future, but the headaches were gone, and his shoulder... He rotated his arm experimentally. "Shoulder is good as new."

This time she snorted.

He laughed. "Really. And no, I haven't forgotten that it will be more susceptible to a dislocation if I get hammered by an avalanche again, but I'm hoping to avoid that."

"Me, too," she said quietly. It was a minute before she asked about Krasnitskiy, although she didn't remember the name.

No, Zach realized, he'd never told her any of the names, only the nationality claimed by the passports they carried.

"He's not up to talking yet, but it looks like

he'll make it. He'll even keep his fingers and toes."

"You bundled him up well."

"Yeah." Uncomfortable with the implication that he was a good man, Zach cleared his throat again.

Behind him, someone else did the same even as the curtain rings rattled. It was the nurse, he saw, who looked sternly at him.

"Ms. Brevik needs to sleep. I'm afraid you'll have to leave now."

He didn't move. "I'm not going anywhere. I'll spend the night right here."

She frowned. "That's against—"

Ava said, "Please. I…feel safe with him here."

To her credit, the nurse backed down, but insisted on turning out the light after taking Ava's temperature and pulse, and then reminded her that she could push the button at any time if she required assistance.

The darkness wasn't all that complete, light from the hall seeping around the curtains, but Zach felt himself relax.

"She's right," he murmured. "You need to sleep."

"You, too," she whispered.

"I will. I can sleep anywhere."

If anything, her fingers tightened around his hand. "Do you think…?" She hesitated.

Zach leaned forward. "Do I think?"

"You could lie down with me?" She sounded tentative, and vulnerable. "I'd…sleep better."

Heart squeezing like a fist, he answered in a low voice, "I haven't showered yet."

"I don't care," she whispered.

"Your guard dog will probably kick me out when she sees us, but…yeah. I'd sleep better, too."

While he kicked off his boots and pulled his quarter-zip over his head, Ava shifted herself sideways on the narrow bed. He carefully climbed on, stretched out beside her and helped her find the position they knew worked best— her cast lying across his chest and belly, her head nestled in the hollow beneath his shoulder.

He wanted to sleep like this every night for the rest of his life—minus the cast.

She sighed, squirmed a little and murmured, "Sleep tight."

Smiling, he closed his eyes, refused to let himself think about tomorrow and stayed awake only until he knew from the slowness of her breaths that she was asleep.

AVA AWAKENED WITH vague snippets of memory telling her the nurse had checked on her a number of times, making her answer questions and expressing her disapproval of Zach sharing the hospital bed, but she must have given up and left them each time. He was gone now, although Ava was sure he'd stayed through the night. Her heart sank when she saw the empty chair.

"Breakfast will be here in just a minute," a new nurse told her cheerily. "Do you need to get up first?"

Oh, heavens—she did. That chore completed, she climbed back into bed laboriously, feeling as if she were old and arthritic.

He'll be back, she told herself. That he'd wanted to stay the night meant everything. Today, though, she'd be released from the hospital.

"Do you know where my friend went?" she asked.

"I'm afraid I didn't see him. Nobody was here when I came on."

Ava could only nod. She actually was hungry, and the breakfast looked surprisingly good to her. Scrambled eggs and oatmeal, easy to eat, a slice of whole wheat bread, and tea and orange juice. Her jaw felt better, she decided as she ate. She started to think about practicalities.

Where was her pack? Obviously not here.

None of the clothing in it was clean, but what she'd been wearing—and she had no idea what had become of that—had to be indescribably filthy. Besides, she'd need her wallet, keys, phone. What day was today? Had she missed her return flight home? Probably. Ugh—replacing the ticket would be costly.

Just as she pushed away the tray, Zach appeared around the curtain. A new Zach—clean and freshly shaven, wearing cargos she didn't remember seeing and a long-sleeve, navy blue T-shirt. And he carried her pack slung over his shoulder.

"Oh, thank goodness!" she exclaimed. "I had no idea what happened to my stuff."

She'd almost forgotten how handsome he was beneath the shaggy growth of beard. Hadn't cared. What had mattered was *who* he was.

"Reid's wife offered to wash your clothes." He glanced down at himself. "He and I are close enough in size. He loaned me something to wear."

"I have clean clothes?" What a thing to get stuck on!

His broad grin sent her pulse into double time. "Best thing that's ever happened to you."

She laughed. "Well, not quite."

On a sharp pant, she knew: the best thing

that had ever happened to her was meeting him. The time they'd had together, however fraught with fear and danger it had been.

"So." He set down the pack and sat in the chair. "Do you have a plan?"

"I haven't gotten that far. I just finished breakfast."

He eyed her empty plate, expression dubious, but didn't comment. The silence felt uncomfortable.

Zach rolled his shoulders, which she'd learned was something of a giveaway for him. He had something to say he didn't want to. Was this the *Goodbye, I have to be back at work, you take care of yourself?*

"Will you come home with me?" he asked. "Heal up for another few days? My place isn't fancy, but—"

"I'd love that," she said in a rush. A reprieve. She was ready to seize that with both hands.

"Good." His relaxation was noticeable. "Maybe I should say this first, though. It could be awkward if you're not thinking anything the same."

The leap of hope plummeted like a stone thrown high in the air. She could only nod.

"We haven't known each other very long, but… I don't want to say goodbye to you." His voice was gruff. "You're the most extraordi-

nary woman I've ever met. My life isn't all tha
exciting anymore compared to yours, but…"
He appeared momentarily lost for words. "I've
been falling for you. Hoping you might have
room in your life for me. So we can figure
out—"

His face blurred. To her horror, Ava realized
she was crying. No, sobbing. She snatched up a
corner of the sheet and tried to quell the flood
but failed. Salty tears stung as they found raw
places.

On an exclamation, Zach moved to sit on the
bed and gently lift her until he could wrap her
in his arms and it was his shirt front she was
soaking. His *clean* shirt.

"I'm sorry," he murmured. "Damn, I didn'
mean to upset you. God, Ava. Please quit cry
ing. Please."

"They're happy tears!" she wailed, but he
probably couldn't make out a single word she
said.

Only…he started to laugh. Rocking her
rubbing his cheek against her head. "It's
okay, sweetheart. Damn. You scared me. I
thought—"

She straightened, pulling back enough to
gaze at him through even puffier eyes, know
ing perfectly well how pathetic *she* must look
"I kept telling myself what I felt wasn't real

but it was. It is! I was terrified of having to saying goodbye."

He grabbed a handful of tissues from her bedside table and mopped up her face as tenderly as if she were a baby.

Tossing the tissues, he agreed roughly, "Yeah. Same. I'm…in love with you, Ava. I'll move to Colorado if that's what you want. I can get a job anywhere. I'll hate waving goodbye when you head out on expeditions, but I hope most of them aren't as dangerous as this one. And…maybe sometimes I can go with you."

"We can live here, you know. There's a lot of spectacular country around here. The Puget Sound, the Gulf Islands, mountains everywhere, the rainforest. I didn't leave anything important behind in Colorado. It's just…a place. I don't mind moving."

He absorbed that. "Then, once they let you go, I'll take you home with me. It's, uh, just a rental, but we can buy something we like together. I can afford it. I didn't want to commit when I first took the job."

"Yes." Oh, it hurt to smile, but she felt as if she must be glowing from some inner light. A niggling thought surfaced, though. "You're not in trouble, are you?"

Zach shook his head. "I have an official offer from the border patrol to join."

"Will you?"

He shook his head. "Too close to what I di[d] the last ten years. I never want to go to wa[r] again. Regular policing, that's different."

"I wish you could kiss me."

He bent forward and rested his forehea[d] against hers. "You have no idea how much [I] wish the same. Soon. And...we have time."

"We have time," Ava echoed, her emotion[s] indescribable. She'd never expected to believ[e] in something like forever with a man, but sh[e] had already given Zach her trust, and woul[d] keep giving it. He wasn't a man who'd ever le[t] her down. "I can hardly wait."

* * * * *

Get 3 FREE REWARDS!

We'll send you 2 FREE Books plus a FREE Mystery Gift.

Both the **Harlequin® Desire** and **Harlequin Presents®** series feature compelling novels filled with passion, sensuality and intriguing scandals.

YES! Please send me 2 FREE novels from the Harlequin Desire or Harlequin Presents series and my FREE gift (gift is worth about $10 retail). After receiving them, if I don't wish to receive any more books, I can return the shipping statement marked "cancel." If I don't cancel, I will receive 6 brand-new Harlequin Presents Larger-Print books every month and be billed just $6.30 each in the U.S. or $6.49 each in Canada, a savings of at least 10% off the cover price, or 3 Harlequin Desire books (2-in-1 story editions) every month and be billed just $7.83 each in the U.S. or $8.43 each in Canada, a savings of at least 12% off the cover price. It's quite a bargain! Shipping and handling is just 50¢ per book in the U.S. and $1.25 per book in Canada.* I understand that accepting the 2 free books and gift places me under no obligation to buy anything. I can always return a shipment and cancel at any time by calling the number below. The free books and gift are mine to keep no matter what I decide.

Choose one:
- ☐ **Harlequin Desire** (225/326 BPA GRNA)
- ☐ **Harlequin Presents Larger-Print** (176/376 BPA GRNA)
- ☐ **Or Try Both!** (225/326 & 176/376 BPA GRQP)

Name (please print)

Address   Apt. #

City   State/Province   Zip/Postal Code

Email: Please check this box ☐ if you would like to receive newsletters and promotional emails from Harlequin Enterprises ULC and its affiliates. You can unsubscribe anytime.

Mail to the **Harlequin Reader Service:**
IN U.S.A.: P.O. Box 1341, Buffalo, NY 14240-8531
IN CANADA: P.O. Box 603, Fort Erie, Ontario L2A 5X3

Want to try 2 free books from another series? Call 1-800-873-8635 or visit www.ReaderService.com.

THE NORA ROBERTS COLLECTION

40% OFF!

Get to the heart of happily-ever-after in these Nora Roberts classics! Immerse yourself in the beauty of love by picking up this incredible collection written by, legendary author, Nora Roberts!

YES! Please send me the **Nora Roberts Collection**. Each book in this collection is 40% off the retail price! There are a total of 4 shipments in this collection. The shipments are yours for the low, members-only discount price of $23.96 U.S./$31.16 CDN. each, plus $1.99 U.S./$4.99 CDN. for shipping and handling. If I do not cancel, I will continue to receive four books a month for three more months. I'll pay just $23.96 U.S./$31.16 CDN., plus $1.99 U.S./$4.99 CDN. for shipping and handling per shipment.* I can always return a shipment and cancel at any time.

☐ 274 2595   ☐ 474 2595

Name (please print)

Address   Apt. #

City   State/Province   Zip/Postal Code

Mail to the Harlequin Reader Service:
IN U.S.A.: P.O. Box 1341, Buffalo, NY 14240-8531
IN CANADA: P.O. Box 603, Fort Erie, Ontario L2A 5X3

*Terms and prices subject to change without notice. Prices do not include sales taxes which will be charged (if applicable) based on your state or country of residence. Canadian residents will be charged applicable taxes. Offer not valid in Quebec. All orders subject to approval. Credit or debit balances in a customer's account(s) may be offset by any other outstanding balance owed by or to the customer. Please allow 3 to 4 weeks for delivery. Offer available while quantities last. © 2022 Harlequin Enterprises ULC.
® and ™ are trademarks owned by Harlequin Enterprises ULC.

Your Privacy—Your information is being collected by Harlequin Enterprises ULC, operating as Harlequin Reader Service. To see how we collect and use this information visit https://corporate.harlequin.com/privacy-notice. From time to time we may also exchange your personal information with reputable third parties. If you wish to opt out of this sharing of your personal information, please visit www.readerservice.com/consumerchoice or call 1-800-873-8635. Notice to California Residents—Under California law, you have specific rights to control and access your data. For more information visit https://corporate.harlequin.com/california-privacy.

NORA2022